Praise

"Allow your imagination to soar with Ben-Tzion Spitz's new book, Destiny's Call. Free from the shackles of academic fastidiousness, Spitz successfully paints vivid backdrops to adorn the canvas of the Biblical story. His colorful interpolations expand the reader's viewing lens to explore unchartered terrain and allow a possible glimpse of the grand Biblical landscape."

Gad Dishi, Author, Jacob's Family Dynamics: Climbing the Rungs of the Ladder

"Spitz's great skill is to make biblical life simultaneously strange and familiar; his work is filled with constant delight and discovery. In short, a treasure."

Ilana Epstein, Columnist, The Jerusalem Post

"Spitz's re-imagination of Biblical characters, places and stories is a pleasure to read. Those who study the Bible will be encouraged to revisit their assumptions; those who do not study the Bible will be inspired to do so."

Rabbi Shalom Z. Berger, Ed.D.
The Lookstein Center for Jewish Education, Bar-Ilan University

"Ben-Tzion Spitz has done a remarkable job of making the Bible relevant to contemporary English readers of all religions and faiths."

Judy Labensohn, www.WriteInIsrael.com

"The Jewish religion and culture have always been a part of Europe but in recent years have been disappearing in the background. This book is therefore an important reminder of the Jewish history that should be but isn't well known in Europe. This book should be read by every European."
Egbert Pijfers, Norway

"Destiny's Call is a fascinating read, bringing the Bible to life in a creative and impressive way. The realistic conversations and powerful descriptions make the reader feel like they are experiencing the stories of the Bible first hand. This book is an excellent resource for all curious readers who are looking to learn about our history in an informative yet enjoyable manner."
Yonatan Shai Freedman, Yeshivat Har Etzion

"As a member of the Hisva Turkey Anatolian Side Jewish Community I would like to introduce this book to the most suitable Jewish institutions."
Baruh Mori, Istanbul, Turkey

"I love the way that Spitz manages to set the scene in every story, to the extent that I feel as if I am living in that moment."
Jennifer Kahen, London, United Kingdom

"As Erich Auerbach has famously demonstrated in his *Mimesis*, the Biblical narrative – in contrast with Homer's all-encompassing rhetoric – features frequent gaps, omissions, and obscurities. These lacunae comprise the starting point of the present work, in which Rabbi Spitz presents us with that which Herbert Hunger has termed *etopoiea*: a creative reconstruction of the characters within the narrative, as well as the dialogue that presumably occurred between them. Rabbi Spitz consistently couches his *etopoiea* within a detailed and compelling backdrop of realia of antiquity, lending his stories a strong sense of verisimilitude. Overall, the short stories contained within this volume – with their multifaceted characterizations, original plots, emotionally-fraught relationships, and comic interludes - offer a unique prism with which to view the Biblical story, providing a framework which will be riveting for children, insightful for adults, and which will undoubtedly engender fruitful discussion among readers of all ages."

Dr. Avi Shmidman, lecturer, Department of Hebrew Literature, Bar-Ilan University

Destiny's Call:
Book One - Genesis

Biblical Fiction

Ben-Tzion Spitz

Valiant Publishing

Destiny's Call: Book One – Genesis

Biblical Fiction

Valiant Publishing, 123 Grove Avenue, Suite 208
Cedarhurst, New York 11516-2033, USA

info@valiantpublishing.com
Website: valiantpublishing.com
Author's blog: ben-tzion.com

For schools or bulk orders, contact the author directly at:
bentzispitz@gmail.com

First Edition

1 3 5 7 9 10 8 6 4 2

ISBN 978-1-937623-51-7

Library of Congress Control Number: 2011938908

To God, I dedicate this first fruit

Maps, Timeline and Genealogies

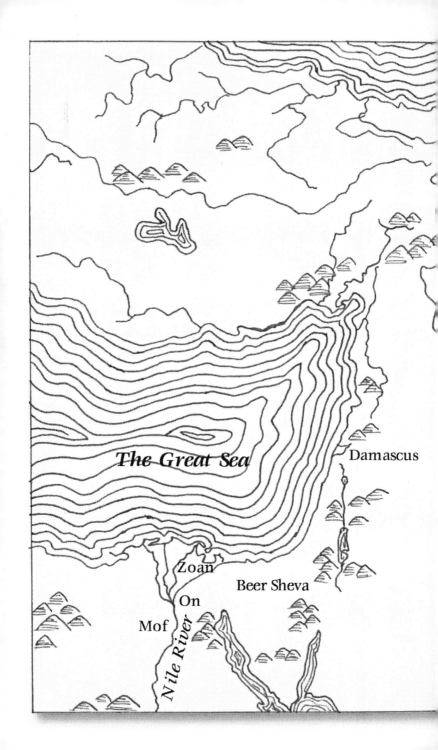

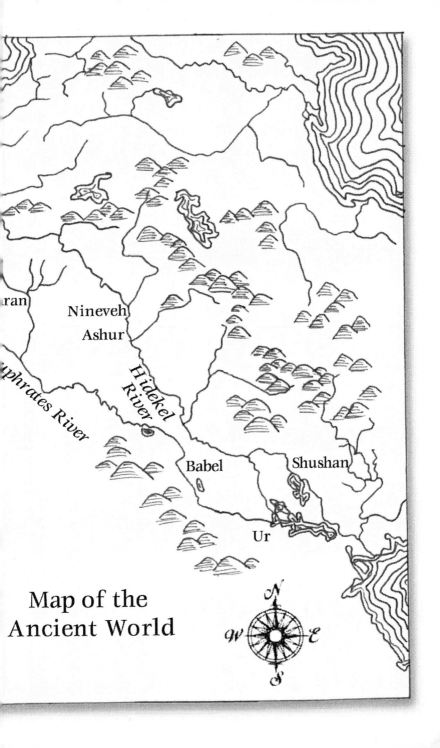

Map of the
Ancient World

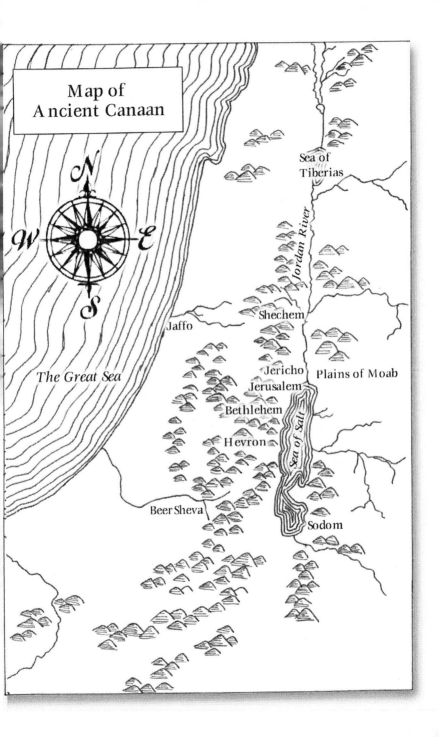

Map of
Ancient Canaan

N
W   E
S

Sea of
Tiberias

Jordan River

Jaffo

Shechem

The Great Sea

Jericho   Plains of Moab
Jerusalem
Bethlehem

Hevron   Sea of Salt

Beer Sheva

Sodom

TIMELINE OF BIBLICAL PERSONALITIES AND EVENTS

<u>*STORY TIMELINE*</u>

FORGE OF MUSIC
(MUCH EARLIER,
PRE-FLOOD)

HEBREW YEARS
GREGORIAN YEARS

<u>BIBLICAL EVENT</u>

ABRAHAM
(1948-2123)

1950
-1810

TOWER OF BABEL
TOWER OF EGOTISM

2000
-1760

OATH-BROTHERS

ESCAPE FROM SODOM

ISAAC
(2048-2228)

2050
-1710

BINDING OF ISAAC

JACOB
(2108-2255)

2100
-1660

RECONCILIATION

2150
-1610

REBECCA'S CRISIS
THE SHEPHERD'S KISS

JACOB AT LAVAN

JOSEPH
(2200-2310)

RACHEL'S GAMBIT
DEATH PANGS

JOSEPH'S EGYPTIAN ATTORNEY

2200
-1560

BENJAMIN'S FEAR
JOSEPH REVEALED

2250
-1510

2300
-1460

THE FIRST ANTI-SEMITE

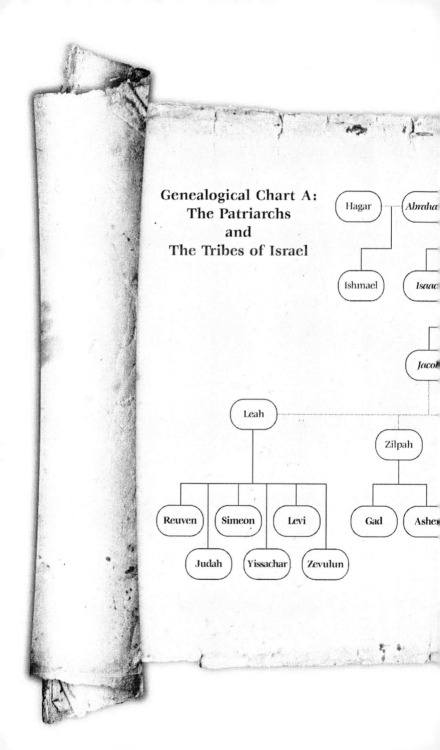

Genealogical Chart A:
The Patriarchs
and
The Tribes of Israel

Hagar — Abraha[m]

Ishmael — Isaac

Jaco[b]

Leah

Zilpah

Reuven — Simeon — Levi

Gad — Ashe[r]

Judah — Yissachar — Zevulun

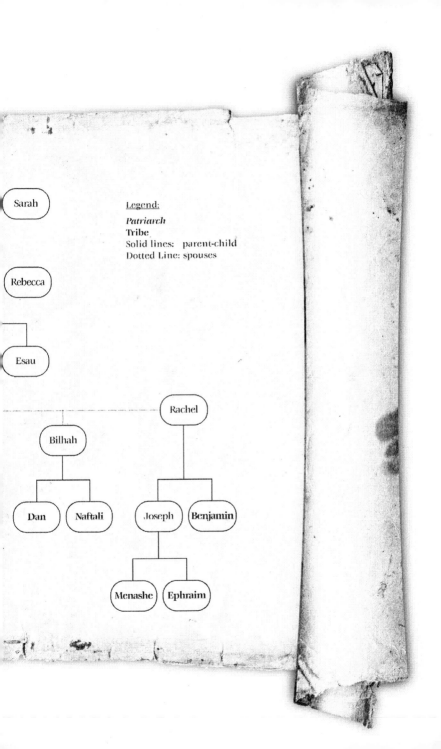

Sarah

Rebecca

Esau

Rachel

Bilhah

Dan   Naftali   Joseph   Benjamin

Menashe   Ephraim

Legend:

Patriarch
Tribe
Solid lines: parent-child
Dotted Line: spouses

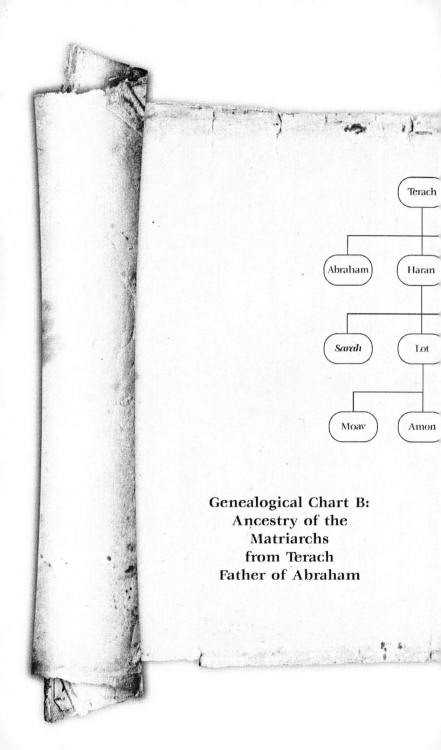

Terach

Abraham   Haran

Sarah   Lot

Moav   Amon

**Genealogical Chart B:
Ancestry of the
Matriarchs
from Terach
Father of Abraham**

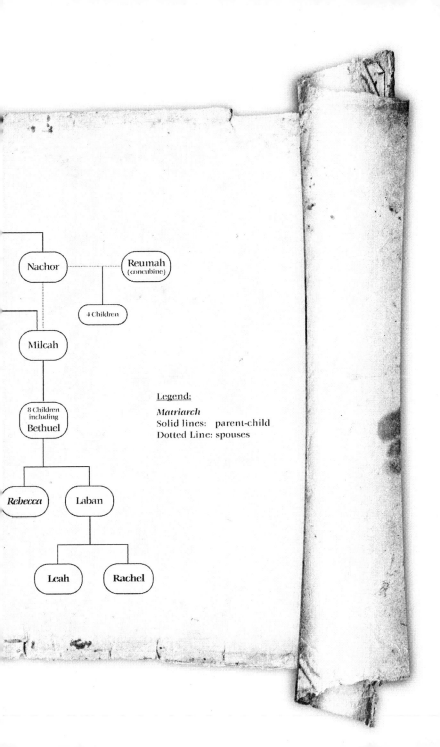

Nachor············Reumah
                  (concubine)

4 Children

Milcah

8 Children
including
Bethuel

Rebecca   Laban

Leah   Rachel

Legend:

Matriarch
Solid lines: parent-child
Dotted Line: spouses

Note on book format and content rights:

Biblical translations are based on the JPS 1917 English translation, courtesy of mechon-mamre.org.

Translations of secondary sources were done freely from the original Hebrew and Aramaic.

Jewish tradition dictates reading on a weekly basis a portion from the Five Books of Moses. Over the course of a yearly cycle, the Pentateuch, as it is also known, is completed.

The page preceding each story has a prominent Hebrew title. The title corresponds to the portion of the week from which each story is drawn (except for "Vayetze" which has two stories).

The story illustrations are from free-domain paintings or woodcuts, some of them hundreds of years old.

Hebrew 'Qumran' font purchased from masterfont.co.il

Table of Contents

[Bereshit]

(Genesis Chapters I-VI)

Two Blacksmiths
Medieval Woodcut

The Forge of Music

"**Yuval!** Cease that infernal noise!" Lemech bellowed in the tool-filled smithy.

"My apologies, Father," Yuval responded meekly, "the spirit of music possessed me again."

"Nonsense," retorted Lemech, "are you a man? Or are you an animal that cannot control itself? Your constant banging is driving me mad," he continued angrily. "Besides, it will ruin our tools and is a distraction from our work."

"Yes, Sir," Yuval mumbled, looking down as he examined the molding he was setting. They were preparing for the production of cooking pots.

Lemech eagerly returned his attention to the molten copper in his furnace, making sure the color reached a precise reddish hue. Lemech had the broad build and darkened skin of a master blacksmith, and could practically manufacture metal by instinct. Nevertheless, he still needed to inspect the coloring. The specific hue of red signified the ideal moment for pouring the flowing metal into the mold.

Suddenly Lemech heard a tapping sound with an unfamiliar rhythm. As he realized the source of the disturbing noise, his blood began to boil. He could not believe his son would continue banging after receiving such strong admonition.

Through clenched teeth, Lemech turned to Yuval and whispered in a deadly tone: "By the Cursed One - your disruptions are becoming unforgivable!"

Lemech then started to pour the copper from the furnace into the mold, but it was too late. The copper had passed the right color. Lemech's anger became explosive. "Fool of a son!" he roared, "you have cost us good metal and an entire day of work!"

"You are good for nothing!" he continued, his anger overcoming his senses. He menacingly raised the molding with the liquid metal still in it. "You add nothing but distress and troubles!"

Yuval stepped back from his father's threatening moves and grabbed a nearby pan to afford himself some protection.

Lemech tripped and the molding, with its red hot contents, went flying towards Yuval.

Yuval instinctively raised the pan to cover his face from the molten copper. The copper fell on his shoulders and chest, immediately combusting his clothing. However, part of the copper bounced off of Yuval's pan right into Lemech's face.

Primal screams erupted from Lemech's workshop.

Lemech's eyes had not been burned completely, but enough so that he could barely see shadows. It took several weeks before Lemech, now the Blind Blacksmith, would enter his forge again.

Yuval had recovered quickly from his superficial burns and had dedicated himself exclusively to the blacksmithing. There were already rumors going about that Yuval's creations were even better than Lemech's renowned work. It was reported that Yuval had also started producing many more wooden tools and wasn't predominantly focused on metal, as Lemech had been. However, there were also rumors that Yuval was creating tools that no man had ever made before and that apparently served no purpose.

Lemech's youngest son, Tuval-Kayin, became his eyes. Over the course of a few weeks at home, they had developed a rapport. With minimal guidance by Tuval-Kayin, Lemech could move around and function again. The big test, however, would come in the smithy.

As Lemech approached the workshop, he already knew something was wrong. Sounds that were not natural to metalworking were emanating from the forge. Not the sound of the roaring furnace, nor that of a hammer on an anvil, nor even the sound of delicate metalwork. It was a sound unlike any Lemech had ever heard, and it was not produced by man.

It had the rhythm of clapping, or even whistling or song, but it was not man-made. It sounded as if it were made by a tool.

Lemech, in hand with Tuval-Kayin, rushed to the smithy.

"Yuval!" Lemech asked in a mixture of anger and confusion. "What is that sound?"

"What sound father?" Yuval asked, taken aback by his father's sudden intrusion.

"That sound I just heard."

"Nothing, Father. Just the wind rattling some of the hanging tools."

"Do not play the fool with me, son. I ought to kill you for your insolence."

"You tried that already father," Yuval said quietly, with both fear and resentment in his voice, "and it did not turn out so well for you."

Lemech was about to charge towards the sound of Yuval's voice, but froze mid-stride. After a moment's pause he said:

"My intention was never to hurt you," Lemech explained haltingly, "my temper got the best of me, and the rest was an unfortunate accident."

Yuval remained silent.

"Hmph," Lemech breathed out, breaking the silence. "Let us move on then. Show me what you have been working on."

Yuval placed a new pot in Lemech's hands.

Lemech touched, caressed, and weighed the pot in his thick hands, as a jeweler would examine a diamond.

"Give me one of my old pots." Lemech requested.

Lemech repeated the procedure. After having inspected all of the new items with silent admiration, Lemech inquired:

"Is there anything else you have been working on?"

"Like what?" Yuval answered defensively.

"Enough, Yuval! Stop playing games with me. Just show me what you have."

Out of instinctive obedience, Yuval handed him an instrument.

Lemech inspected the instrument with his hands for a long time before speaking. He perceived a wooden frame covered with plated bronze on the edges. Lemech counted with his seeing fingers ten strings drawn across the frame. The combination of wood, metal and string was one he had never dreamed of, let alone understood.

"What is it?"

"I call it a lyre. It plays music."

Lemech started to laugh from surprise. It was a deep rumbling laugh that radiated from his torso.

"No. Truly, Yuval. What does this contraption do?"

"Father, the instrument you are holding, when touched a certain way, makes musical notes that cannot be copied by man. When played in certain sequences it can be quite beautiful."

"Show me."

Yuval took the instrument back and ran his fingers across the strings.

At first he played a soothing melody, followed by a dramatic piece full of anger, love and passion. He ended with a light wistful score that spoke of dreams unfulfilled.

Lemech was dumbstruck. For several moments he did not move at all. Then big salty tears streamed down his scarred face. He started crying.

He sat his large bulk down on the smithy floor and began to sob uncontrollably.

After a few minutes he composed himself. He raised his towering figure up again, facing Yuval.

"Yuval," he said, with a voice no one had ever heard before.

"Yes, Father," replied Yuval in apprehension.

"What you have created is magical. I was a blind and arrogant fool not to appreciate your musical inclination before."

"I am sorry as well father, for being the cause of your physical blindness."

"Do not be. I am finally able to see clearly. My wounds are self-inflicted. But that is enough time spent on remorse. We have work to do."

"Yes, Father. What would you like to do?"

"Why, we have lots of pots and pans, and hammers and hoes, and spears and arrowheads and many more things to make."

Yuval was crestfallen at the verdict. He died a small death, but walked back to the furnace with resignation.

But Lemech continued: "And I would also like you to show me how you make those clever musical instruments of yours."

Biblical Sources:

Genesis 4:17-21

"And Cain knew his wife, and she conceived and bore Enoch. He (Cain) became a city-builder, and named the city after his son Enoch. To Enoch was born Irad, and Irad begot Mehuyael, and Mehuyael begot Methushael, and Methushael begot Lemech.

Lemech took to himself two wives: The name of one was Adah, and the name of the second was Zillah. And Adah bore Yaval; he was the founder of those who dwell in tents and breed cattle. The name of his brother was **Yuval; he was the founder of all who handle the harp and flute."**

[Noah]

(Genesis Chapters VI-XI)

THE CONFUSION OF TONGUES

And they said, Go to, let us build us a city and a tower, whose top may reach unto heaven . . . So the Lord scattered them abroad from thence upon the face of all the earth . . . (Genesis 11: 4,8)   (11 : 14)

Gustave Doré (1832-1883)

Tower of Egotism

Nimrod jumped the steps of The Tower three at a time with powerful, energetic strides. He stood at the top of The Tower just as the first rays of sunrise shone on it. The entire populace for miles around saw his large, muscular frame capping the monstrously imposing structure. He ushered in the new day and formalized his status as King and God.

Nimrod's priests offered conventional sacrifices and libations. The smell of burning animal fat and incense filled the air. He strode to a room below the top of The Tower where he consumed a sumptuous breakfast of bread, beef, eggs and vegetables with a savage appetite. He ate in front of his lieutenants and servants, all awaiting his slightest fancy. Satiated, content and surveying his empire, Nimrod allowed his lieutenants to report on activity and issues of the day. Nimrod gestured towards a tall thin man standing at the front of his lieutenants, Mebtah.

"Your Majesty," Mebtah, his Chief Lieutenant, bowed deeply, "all the workgroups are falling behind on the scheduled milestones. I have personally investigated each group and witnessed that their productivity has indeed deteriorated. My concern is that their efforts will decline further. We may not complete the full structure of The Tower before the autumn rains."

"This is highly disturbing," Nimrod stated menacingly. "What do you propose?"

"My conclusion, your Majesty," Mebtah continued unperturbed, "is that we permit the requested weekly day of rest. Let me provide an example. This brick," Mebtah held out in his thin right hand a solid and attractive looking brick, "was produced early in our construction. I took the liberty of keeping it as a model for future construction. However, this brick," and now Mebtah held out his equally thin left hand, demonstrating an ugly, ill-shaped and frail looking piece, "this brick, was produced yesterday."

"I see. And how will a day of rest solve this problem? I would think it would delay us further," the King asked, the frown on his ruddy face growing.

"Yes, your Majesty," Mebtah replied, "a day of rest does seem at first to go against reason. However, I believe that the main cause for the poor effort is that we are pushing the workers too hard. If they have a chance to recuperate on a consistent basis, I am certain we shall see an improvement in productivity."

"What will happen if you are wrong, Mebtah?"

"I am not. But even if I were, we would at most lose a day of work, your Majesty."

"And what solutions could we try then?"

"We would need some way to work them harder, motivate them further."

Nimrod sat pensively for a few minutes, looking at Mebtah, looking at the distance, and looking at the workers doing their tasks throughout The Tower and on the ground below.

He stood up suddenly, like an animal about to pounce on his prey.

"Mebtah, I cannot take the chance that you are wrong."

"I understand, your Majesty."

"We must complete The Tower before the rains."

"I agree completely."

"To show softness at this critical time would have a negative effect on morale."

"Um, perhaps, your Majesty."

"Mebtah, you have been a loyal and dedicated Lieutenant." Nimrod stated with an ironic grimace on his face.

"Yes, your Majesty." Mebtah was suddenly confused, not following his lieges' thinking as he usually did.

"You would give your life at my command without hesitation?" Nimrod asked, his grin getting broader.

"Why, of course, your Majesty." Mebtah replied slowly, feeling as if a trap had been sprung on him, but still not seeing its contours.

"Then you will understand what I am about to do."

And without further delay, Nimrod vigorously grabbed the tall but thin Mebtah. Nimrod held on to the belt by Mebtah's waist and the garment by his shoulder, and hoisted Mebtah over his head. To Nimrod, Mebtah was as light as a puppet in a child's hands. Nimrod then climbed with Mebtah to the top of The Tower. Mebtah, his eyes wild and confused, held on tightly to the bricks in either hand, almost in a death-grip.

At the top of The Tower, with Mebtah over his head, Nimrod called out in a booming voice.

"My people!"

"My people!"

"Heed the words of your ruler!"

16

"The man I hold in my hands is Mebtah, my loyal Chief Lieutenant."

"He feels that we cannot complete our Tower in time."

"He is wrong, and his lack of faith is offensive to the Gods."

"This is what happens to those that do not work hard, or do not obey the Gods."

Nimrod, with great flourish and drama, proceeded to throw Mebtah from the roof of the tower. The eyes of every single worker were on Mebtah's body. The descent seemed to take forever, yet the resounding, sickening thud occurred all too quickly.

Within moments, the workers started scurrying like ants and returned to their tasks with renewed vigor and energy.

Nimrod nonchalantly turned to two of his other lieutenants and said:

"Make sure to bring up Mebtah's two bricks for me."

They raced down, each eager to get the bricks first.

Biblical Sources:

Genesis 10:8-10

8. And Cush begot Nimrod; he began to be a mighty one in the earth. 9. He was a mighty hunter before the Lord; wherefore it is said: 'Like Nimrod a mighty hunter before the Lord.' 10 And the beginning of his kingdom was Babel, and Erech, and Accad, and Calneh, in the land of Shinar.

Secondary Sources:

Babylonian Talmud, Tractate Chulin 89a

"God gave renown to Nimrod, nevertheless, he said, *''Come, let us build us a city, and a tower, with its top in heaven...'* (Genesis 11:4)"

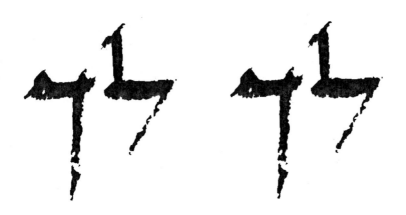

[Lech Lecha]

(Genesis Chapters XII – XVII)

Malchizedek Blesses Abram
Henry Davenport Northrop (1894)

Oath-Brothers

"I shall not go with Abram on this crazed campaign," Eshkol stomped his long but lithe feet on the intricately tiled floor of Mamre's home, "it is suicide!"

"How can you even think to abandon us, Eshkol?" Mamre responded from deep within his barrel chest. "You would sunder our sacred covenant with Abram, out of cowardice?"

Aner, the eldest of the three, who had been watching the debate with growing concern, stood up to intercept Eshkol before he got within striking distance of Mamre.

"Now, now, Mamre," Aner asserted in soothing tones, as he grabbed on to Eshkol, "there is no need to speak so disparagingly of our brother."

"Mamre, we have fought side by side with Abram on previous skirmishes and small raids," Eshkol said more tersely, standing a bit taller, "where I was very much in danger and threatened personally. But what Abram proposes now is nothing less than suicide. To attack Amrafel's legions, after they successfully destroyed the combined armies of Sodom and Gemorah, is simply insane. We are speaking of pitting our workers and slaves against Amrafel's professional soldiers."

"Do not try to frighten me," Mamre answered angrily, "I am loyal to the death to Abram, and more importantly to the God of Abram, who visibly protects him like a favored child. Abram must rescue his nephew from Amrafel, and we, his oath-brothers, must go with him. The God who protects and blesses Abram will continue to protect and bless us as well."

"I too believe in his God," Eshkol explained. "However, against such a formidable foe, we might as well take our own lives here at home – we would save ourselves the journey, and Abram's God the hassle."

Aner cleared his throat, getting both Mamre's and Eshkol's attention. "I too am fearful of such a momentous undertaking. However, we cannot forsake our brother Abram."

"By placing us in such an impossible position," Eshkol retorted, "Abram is the one who is forsaking us. I shall not throw away my life against all reason."

"First," Mamre stuck out a beefy finger, his voice getting louder again, "Abram has not called us to help him. Second, Abram, our great brother, would not think any less of any of us for not joining him. Third, and most importantly – you are lacking in faith. Faith! If you do not have the faith that the God of Abram, the One and Only God, as Abram has taught us; that the Creator and Ruler of the Earth, can perform miracles beyond our imagination – then perhaps you are better off staying home. Though I think it would break my heart and perhaps our friendship." Mamre then sat down heavily, looking away from his guests.

Eshkol stood speechless. His mouth hung open at Mamre's statements. He too sat down morosely. After a few silent moments he uncomfortably explained:

"It may be true that my fear is greater than my faith. However, I cannot live with my friendship being questioned. I just require some more tangible hope - something concrete that will let reason rule over trepidation."

Eshkol's confession was greeted with an awkward silence.

"Then let me suggest a thought you just inspired," Aner broke the quiet, "that encourages me and may give you the concrete loadstone you require. Amrafel has just re-conquered and ransacked the entire plain of our very wealthy neighbors of Sodom and Gemorah. If by some miracle the God of Abram were to place Amrafel in our hands, the spoils of this war would be beyond anything we have ever seen."

"That is indeed a more tangible goal," Eshkol stated more excitedly, "though equally suicidal."

"The spoils would be ours by convention," Mamre added, "and they would indeed be monumental. Though that is not what ultimately draws me, and I am sure it holds little allure for Abram."

"But it is agreed then," the elder Aner looked meaningfully at thin Eshkol, "we are in this to-gether, with the explicit understanding that we get our fair share of the spoils."

Eshkol looked pensively at Aner and then at the brooding Mamre. He was in mortal fear of attacking Amrafel's legions. The image of facing Amrafel's army made his legs wobble and his stomach churn. But he could not face the possibility of being branded a coward. Such a mark would ruin him. And the thought of disappointing Mamre, and even worse, the holy Abram, was more than he could bear. How could he abandon his friends, his oath-brothers? They had always been there for him, especially Abram. Abram was so kind, gentle and wise, yet so strong, firm and courageous. He knew in his heart he would follow Abram to the ends of the earth.

Old Aner was right. The idea of the spoils was a good distraction and lessened the dread. And Mamre was right too. The God of Abram had performed miracles for Abram against all odds. He was indeed powerful.

"I am with you." Eshkol declared emotionally. "I was wrong to even sow doubt in our friendship."

Mamre leapt up with a tear in his eye. "My dear Eshkol," Mamre almost cried as he grabbed Eshkol's forearm, "I am sorry I even questioned your friendship. This will be a grand adventure."

At that very moment, as if by divine inspiration, Abram walked in to Mamre's house.

Aner was the first to greet him and quickly pulled Abram into the embrace of Eshkol and Mamre.

"All hail Abram!" Aner exclaimed, "Prince of God!"

"All hail Abram! Prince of God!" Eshkol and Mamre responded.

"We are with you in all your troubles. Be strong and of good courage!" Aner sang.

"We are with you in all your troubles." Eshkol and Mamre rejoined in unison.

"Be strong and of good courage!"

Biblical Sources:

Genesis Chapter 14

1. And it came to pass in the days of Amrafel king of Shinar, Arioch king of Ellasar, Chedorlaomer king of Elam, and Tidal king of Goiim, 2. that they made war with Bera king of Sodom, and with Birsha king of Gomorrah, Shinab king of Admah, and Shemeber king of Zeboiim, and the king of Bela--the same is Zoar. 3. All these came as allies unto the vale of Siddim--the same is the Salt Sea. 4. Twelve years they served Chedorlaomer, and in the thirteenth year they rebelled. 5. And in the fourteenth year came Chedorlaomer and the kings that were with him, and smote the Rephaim in Ashteroth-karnaim, and the Zuzim in Ham, and the Emim in Shaveh-kiriathaim, 6. and the Horites in their mount Seir, unto El-paran, which is by the wilderness. 7. And they turned back, and came to En-mishpat--the same is Kadesh--and smote all the country of the Amalekites, and also the Amorites, that dwelt in Hazazon-tamar. 8. And there went out the king of

Sodom, and the king of Gemorah, and the king of Admah, and the king of Zeboiim, and the king of Bela--the same is Zoar; and they set the battle in array against them in the vale of Siddim;

9. Against Chedorlaomer king of Elam, and Tidal king of Goiim, and Amrafel king of Shinar, and Arioch king of Ellasar; four kings against the five. 10. Now the vale of Siddim was full of slime pits; and the kings of Sodom and Gemorah fled, and they fell there, and they that remained fled to the mountain. 11. And they took all the goods of Sodom and Gemorah, and all their victuals, and went their way. 12. And they took Lot, Abram's brother's son, who dwelt in Sodom, and his goods, and departed. 13. And there came one that had escaped, and told Abram the Hebrew--now he dwelt by the terebinths of Mamre the Amorite, brother of Eshkol, and brother of Aner; and these were confederate with Abram. 14. And when Abram heard that his brother was taken captive, he led forth his trained men, born in his house, three hundred and eighteen, and pursued as far as Dan. 15. And he divided himself against them by night, he and his servants, and smote them, and pursued them unto Hobah, which is on the left hand of Damascus. 16. And he brought back all the goods, and also brought back his brother Lot, and his goods, and the women also, and the

people. 17. And the king of Sodom went out to meet him, after his return from the slaughter of Chedorlaomer and the kings that were with him, at the vale of Shaveh--the same is the King's Vale. 18. And Malchizedek king of Salem brought forth bread and wine; and he was priest of God the Most High. 19. And he blessed him, and said: 'Blessed be Abram of God Most High, Maker of heaven and earth; 20. And blessed be God the Most High, who hath delivered your enemies into thy hand.' And he gave him a tenth of all. 21. And the king of Sodom said unto Abram: 'Give me the persons, and take the goods to thyself.'22. And Abram said to the king of Sodom: 'I have lifted up my hand unto the Lord, God Most High, Maker of heaven and earth, 23. That I will not take a thread nor a shoe-latchet nor aught that is yours, lest thou should say: I have made Abram rich; 24. Save only that which the young men have eaten, and the portion of the men which went with me, Aner, Eshkol, and Mamre, let them take their portion.'

Secondary Sources:

Bereshit Rabbah 42:8

At the time that the Holy One, Blessed be He, commanded Abraham to circumcise himself, he went and asked advice from his three friends…

Eshkol cautioned him, "Why would you allow your enemies to destroy you, (mitigated by circumcision, you will be unable to prevent their attack)?" The Holy One, Blessed be He, responded: "By your life, I will not present myself to Abraham in the dwelling place of Eshkol…"

Aner warned him, "You are a hundred years old at present, and you are going to afflict yourself with pain?"

Mamre opined to him, "Your Lord Who protected you in the fiery furnace, in the conflict with the kings, and in times of scarcity – will you not abide by Him when He commands you to circumcise yourself?" The Holy One, Blessed be He, said to Mamre, "You encouraged him to circumcise himself – by your life, I will present myself to him only in your dwelling place." *'And the LORD appeared unto him by the terebinths of Mamre'* (Genesis 18:1)

[Vayera]

(Genesis Chapters XVIII-XXII)

THE FLIGHT OF LOT

Then the Lord rained upon Sodom and upon Gomorrah brimstone and fire from
the Lord out of heaven...his [Lot's] wife looked back from behind him, and she became a pillar of salt...(Genesis 19: 24, 26)   (19 -)

Gustave Doré (1832-1883)

Escape from Sodom

"Get your hand off of me!" Edis shrieked at Archangel Michael.

Michael did not pay any attention to Edis. With an inhuman single-mindedness, Michael took the hands of Lot and his wife, Edis, and proceeded to walk them briskly out of the city of Sodom, under the darkly overcast sky.

Archangel Gabriel was doing the same with Lot's youngest daughters. Madis, the older of the two, was on his right, and Atis, the youngest, on his left. Each girl was firmly in hand, unable to escape the iron grasp and unable to do anything but keep pace with the rapidly moving angel.

Lot's two older daughters, standing beside their husbands, looked on in disbelief as the strange procession quickly moved away from the courtyard of Lot's house.

"Where are you going?" Shutis, the oldest, called out.

"We are leaving - now!" Lot called back hastily, "Sodom will be destroyed any minute."

"I just need to gather a few more things and I will catch up with you," Shutis promised, while her husband could be heard giggling in incomprehension.

"No!" Lot demanded, "there is no time. Come with us right now or you will be lost!"

"Remember to bring my jeweled hairpin!" Edis offered hopefully to her daughter.

Shutis quickly ran back into the house and was out of earshot.

"We are going to destroy the entire plain," Gabriel explained in a neutral tone, keeping up the fast pace.

"Please. Please wait for the rest of my family," Lot pleaded.

"It is too late," Gabriel stated with a firm finality, "they are more interested in their material possessions than in their lives."

"What are you talking about?" Edis asked angrily. "They are coming right along. And the things they are bringing are important."

"You do not understand, woman. The sins of these cities are so great that God could not delay destroying them any longer. And destroy them we shall. Utterly. Nothing shall remain of what you knew as Sodom. If it were not for the merit of your uncle Abraham, you too would now die in the city."

They arrived outside the gates of the city.

Michael and Gabriel simultaneously released their captives.

Gabriel raised his hands to the sky. The dark clouds rumbled. Thunder and lightning cracked the thick air. The sky detonated as if the long-foretold end-of-the-world had arrived. The angry sky poured fiery stones and acidic rain. Lot and his family heard panic and screams from inside the city. A crescendo of shrieks forced Lot's daughters to cover their ears. An acrid smell of burning flesh filled the air.

Michael spoke to Lot's family with a booming voice that resonated to the heavens.

"Flee for your lives! Do not look behind you or stop anywhere in all the plain; flee to the mountain lest you be swept away."

Michael raised his hand and a beam of light erupted from his fingertips. The light reached the side of the mountain. Rock and earth exploded, sending fragments in all directions. The mountain was shrouded by a cloud of debris. After moments, the dust settled. To their complete astonishment, Lot and his family saw the contours of a road. The road was the straightest and smoothest road they had ever seen. It led straight up the mountain - to Abraham.

Lot loved his uncle, but could never return to him again. In his uncle's shadow he would always be lesser. The sinner. The bad one. Repugnant. Worthless. He would die before he returned to Abraham. No. He needed to escape elsewhere. Now.

Lot fell to his knees and begged. "Please, no! My Lord – see, now, your servant has found grace in your eyes, and your kindness which you did with me to save my life was great, but I cannot escape to the mountain lest the evil attach itself to me and I die. Behold, please, this city is near enough to escape," Lot pointed further up the plain, "and it is small." Lot's voice started to break. "I shall flee there. Is it not small? – and I will live."

Michael stood pensively for a moment and then replied:

"Behold, I have granted you consideration even regarding this, that I not overturn the city about which you have spoken. Hurry, flee there, for I cannot do a thing until you arrive there."

Michael raised his hand towards the city that would be called Zoar. Light radiated from his hand and tore through the rolling fields of grass and pasture. On the uphill slope to Zoar, Michael had again created a road.

Michael then vanished into thin air, while Gabriel continued to rain down fire and brimstone on Sodom.

The heat behind them increased. Lot grabbed his daughters and yelled to Edis: "Edis, let us go. Let us save at least these two children."

The family walked briskly but mechanically up the hill, through a thickening fog of ash. They were in shock, not understanding what was occurring.

The girls were the first to start crying. They slowed down.

Lot continued to pull them by the hand. "Madis. Atis. Let us go. We must keep on moving. And whatever you do – do not look back!"

The wails from Sodom were reaching a fevered pitch. The scent of fire and burned flesh was overwhelming. Then the screams quieted down. Finally it was silent. Ominously quiet.

Edis cried quietly, tears flowing down her soot-covered face. She slowly repeated: "My babies. My poor babies."

She looked at Lot, walking in front of her with the two girls. Her anguish turned to confusion and then to anger.

She lunged for Lot, knocking him to the ground. She punched him on the back with her fists.

"It is all your fault!" Edis sobbed hysterically. "My babies are dead! My jewels gone! Why did you have to invite those beings in? You are always trying to be better than everyone else. Superior! You and your morality! You are a filthy, lustful leech just like everyone else! But look at what you have done! Look at what you have done!!"

Madis and Atis quickly grabbed their mother from either side and gently lifted her off of Lot. Lot got back on his feet and looked at Edis tenderly.

"I am sorry, Edis, but it is not my fault. The Sodomites were so immoral that it was inevitable that they would be punished. I did what I could, but it was not enough. The chiefs of Sodom sneered and threatened me when I raised even a hint of kindness." Lot bowed his head. "I am sorry for our children. They too would not listen. We tried."

"Sorry?! Tried?!" Edis asked, mad with grief. "You sniveling excuse of a man. I will go back and find them."

"Edis." Lot said very firmly, clasping her arm. "We cannot go back. We cannot even look back or we will surely die."

Instinctively, Madis and Atis positioned themselves behind their mother to prevent her from going backwards, and to block her view if she turned.

Edis abruptly ripped her arm out of Lot's grip. "How dare you tell me what to do? My wealth is destroyed. My babies may be dead back home, or they might be following us right now, and you are too cowardly to save them - to even turn around and check? I will go myself if I have to."

"Mother! No!" Madis grabbed her mother from behind. "Did you not hear the angel? Everyone is dead. I can feel the heat getting closer. If we do not continue, if we even look back, we will die!"

"How can I go on?" Edis was sobbing uncontrollably. "My babies are dead. My husband is no husband. Where will we go? What about my house, my jewelry, and my friends? I must return."

Edis started to slip out of Madis' embrace. Atis saw the movement and she tried to grab her mother and block her view. But Edis was quicker. She turned around, now embraced on either side by her daughters, and took a full frontal look at the destruction of Sodom.

She could not believe her eyes. The lush fields. The strong walls. The rich houses. The colorful courtyards. They were completely destroyed. The entire plain was blackened and distorted. Thick black smoke covered the entire sky. The only color in the world was the red of angry flames, consuming the dead remains of a once proud civilization.

Then she understood. She understood that Sodom was completely evil. She understood that she was an active participant and she knew that she too deserved to die.

Salty tears poured freely down her face, pooling around her feet.

The tingling started in her toes. They became numb. The feeling spread quickly up her legs. Edis gasped in shock and looked down at her legs. Madis and Atis jumped back and stared in disbelief at what seemed like salt replacing their mother's skin. Edis could taste the salt in her mouth as the metamorphosis worked its way up her torso. Edis' feeling of horror was mirrored on the faces of her daughters.

"MOTHER!!" they cried in unison, grabbing her again, as if by embracing her they could stop the process.

Edis had time for only three words before the transformation was complete.

"I am sorry." she whispered with her last tears.

And then she was a pillar of salt.

Biblical Sources:

Genesis Chapter 19

Secondary Sources:

Pirkei d'Rabbi Eliezer 25
"Lot's wife was named Edis."

Targum Yonatan, Bereshit 19:26
"She was a local of Sodom."

Bereshit Rabbah 50:9
"He had four daughters: two were engaged and two were married."

Bereshit Rabbah 50:10
"The angels hastened Lot" (Genesis 19:15). An angel flattened the road in front of them to accelerate Lot's escape."

Bereshit Rabbah 51:5

"She visited the neighbors with the pretense of needing salt and said, "We ourselves are not lacking salt; boarders are staying with us." In this way the people of Sodom learned about the angels. Therefore, she was transformed into salt."

Bava Metzia 86b

"The angel Gabriel departed to destroy Sodom, and Michael to rescue Lot."

Yalkut Shimoni, Vayeira 84

"I cannot flee to the mountain." (Genesis 19:19) While I lived in Sodom, the Holy One, Blessed be He, noted my conduct and the conduct of those in my town, and I was honorable in comparison. If I go forthwith to Abraham, whose great actions are far more abundant than mine, I will not be able to stand up to his burning coal [i.e., I will be judged as corrupt in comparison and will be castigated]"

Midrash Hagadol, Bereshit 19:26

"The wife of Lot, Edis, was overcome with concern for her married daughters in Sodom, and she peered back to see if they were pursuing her.

[Chaye Sarah]

(Genesis Chapters XXIII-XXV)

HAGAR AND ISHMAEL IN THE WILDERNESS

And the angel of God called to Hagar . . . Arise, lift up the lad, for I will make him
a great nation . . . (Genesis 21: 17, 18)

Gustave Doré (1832-1883)

Reconciliation

Though Ishmael was thirteen years Isaac's senior, he still looked more muscular and more vigorous than his scholarly-looking half-brother. Ishmael's decades as a marauder had done nothing to lessen his vitality. The enormous assembly opened a path for Ishmael as he strode confidently, making his way to meet Isaac at the entrance to the Machpela cave, nestled in the Hebron hills.

Isaac had thought about this meeting for some time. He would show the traditional honor to his estranged, exiled older brother.

Ishmael stopped within two paces of Isaac with an unreadable expression on his face. The assembly seemed to be holding its breath, waiting to see how the reunion of the sons of Abraham would unfold.

Isaac outstretched his arms to Ishmael, giving him a light embrace and perfunctory kisses on either cheek. Ishmael reciprocated instinctively, but still held himself tightly.

"Brother," Isaac said formally, bowing his head lightly.

"Brother." Ishmael mirrored the motion.

"It is a great honor to our father that you came to participate in his burial ceremony," Isaac announced.

"Isaac, it is you who honors me by allowing me to participate."

"How could it be any other way? You are his eldest. Please lead us into the cave to commence the ceremony." Isaac beckoned toward the narrow cave opening.

"No, Isaac. You should enter first."

"Father would have wanted me to honor you and let you start the proceedings."

"You honor me by having waited for me and allowing me to participate at all. I am not even deserving of this honor. I have been a disgrace and a blemish to our Father's name. You are his true heir. The world knows this." Ishmael looked Isaac in the eye and then lowered his head.

Isaac reached out to hold Ishmael by the shoulder. "It is true that Father might have been disappointed with your lifestyle, but do not doubt that he ever loved you any less."

Ishmael looked up, his voice heavy with emotion. "That is what is perhaps most painful. He loved me, yet he still exiled me."

"You left him no choice. You threatened to ruin his mission and everything he stood for."

"Now I know. I was too headstrong. I did not understand what he kept telling me. He kept giving me second-chances. I presumed there was no line I could not cross."

"I think that if it had been solely up to Father, he never would have banished you. God gave him a direct command."

"Yes. Father probably should have been firmer with me at an earlier stage, before he had to take such drastic measures. I almost died in the desert."

"God has been with you, in His own way. I do not believe He ever abandoned you, even in the depths of your trouble."

"God has indeed been with me, and He has given me great wealth, children and success in all my undertakings. However, I was not always with God."

"Come then my brother." Isaac tried maneuvering Ishmael towards the entrance. "Lead us into the cave. I can see clearly that you have repented from your ways. God loves the penitent and it would give Father great pleasure for you to initiate the ceremony."

"No," Ishmael said with quiet finality, not budging from his place. "Of this I am adamant and have given much thought. You have been and always will be Father's true heir; you're the son of his beloved soul-mate, Sarah. Whatever claim I might have had as Firstborn, I renounced by turning my back on Father's teachings and ways. While I deeply regret what I have done with my life, and will try to make amends with what remains of it, some things cannot be changed. Some wrongs cannot be righted. The blemishes may never completely heal. You are the true and only heir. Father's faith and mission will run true in your bloodline."

"Are you certain that you wish to relinquish this honor?" Isaac asked tenderly.

"Yes, my brother. Besides, it is disrespectful to both our Father and the assembled multitude for us to debate further."

Isaac squeezed Ishmael's shoulder, and then suddenly embraced him in a strong and long embrace. Tears flowed down both their eyes.

Without another word, Isaac turned around and led the way to the narrow cave entrance, followed closely by Ishmael.

For the first time in their relationship, Isaac felt that his back was not in danger from his brother. In fact, he felt safer.

Biblical Sources:

Genesis Chapter 25: 8-10
8. And Abraham expired, and died in a good old age, an old man, and full of years; and was gathered to his people. 9. And Isaac and Ishmael his sons buried him in the cave of Machpelah, in the field of Ephron the son of Zohar the Hittite, which is before Mamre; 10. the field which Abraham purchased of the children of Heth; there was Abraham buried, and Sarah his wife.

Secondary Sources:

Shemot Rabbah 1:1
As his father Abraham spoilt him and did not chastise him, Ishmael regressed towards a sinful course, until Abraham began to despise him and exiled him from his home, destitute.

Once his father had cast him out, he waited at the intersection and stole from people.

Pirkei d'Rabbi Eliezer 30

His (Ishmael's) mother solicited her father's house and acquired for him a woman called Fatimah. Three years later, Abraham visited his son once more. He arrived at noon and met Ishmael's wife in the house. "Accord me some bread and some water, for my energy is diminished from the journey," he asked. She retrieved the provisions and presented them to him. Abraham rose and entreated the Holy One, Blessed be He, and Ishmael's home became bountiful with many great things. When Ishmael returned, his wife told him what happened, and Ishmael understood that his father still cared for him.

Bereshit Rabbah 62:3

'And Isaac and Ishmael his sons buried him in the cave of Machpelah' (Genesis 25:9). Here Ishmael, the son of the mistress, gave respect to Isaac, the son of the matron, by allowing Isaac to preceed him.

Bereshit Rabbah 62:5

"And these are the years of the life of Ishmael" (Genesis 25:17). Why did the Sacred Writ enumerate the years of a corrupt character? For he travelled a great distance from the desert in order to do a courteous act – to attend the funeral of his father.

Tractate Bava Batra 16b:

Since Ishmael, the firstborn, gave Isaac, his younger brother, precedence, we deduce that he atoned for his sins.

תּוֹלְדוֹת

[Toldot]

(Genesis Chapter XXV-XXVIII)

ISAAC BLESSING JACOB

And Jacob went near unto Isaac his father; and he felt him, and said, The voice
is Jacob's voice, but the hands are the hands of Esau ... (Genesis 27: 22)   (27: 27)

Gustave Doré (1832-1883)

Rebecca's Crisis

The words of the prophecy rang in Rebecca's head. She had held those mysterious words in her heart since before the birth of the twins. They had done nothing to console her pain; they only fueled her confusion and apprehension. She looked towards the entrance of Isaac's tent anxiously, the words reverberating in her mind:

"Two peoples are in your womb;
two nations from your insides shall be separated;
one nation shall strengthen over the other nation,
and the Elder shall serve the Younger."

Rebecca could not bear the tension much longer. Esau, her eldest, was approaching blind Isaac's tent, and after what seemed like an eternity, Jacob, young, sweet Jacob, had not yet exited.

She sat discretely and quietly outside Isaac's tent. Esau brusquely opened the flap of the tent and strode in, but still there was no Jacob. Rebecca held her breath for the imminent explosion. She knew Esau's temper. Esau would immediately understand Jacob's impersonating him, and the charade would be over. The blessings might indeed turn into a curse as Jacob feared, perhaps even violently so.

Then, from within the fold of the tent, Jacob silently stepped out unnoticed and left the area.

Thank You, God. Rebecca thought to herself with great relief. *Jacob received the blessing that Isaac intended for Esau, undiscovered.*

Esau's growing agitation was heard clearly from outside. The confusion emanating from the tent was palpable. And then she heard a blood-curling scream.

"Nooooooo!!!" Esau moaned.

What have I done? Rebecca asked herself.

She could not believe her ears. Her strong, forceful son, Esau, started crying a bitter, deep cry that cut her to the bone. "Have you but one blessing, Father?" Esau pleaded, "Bless me too, Father!"

I am sorry my son. Rebecca told herself. *I had no choice. The prophecy must be fulfilled. You are truly not worthy to succeed Isaac. "The Elder shall serve the Younger."*

Isaac bestowed some makeshift blessing on Esau. Esau left his father's tent in a fury, with murder on his mind. The blood drained from Rebecca's face when she caught a glimpse of his eyes.

He will kill my Jacob. I must warn him. I must get Jacob away from here.

There were a few minutes of silence in the tent, as Isaac composed himself.

"Rebecca, my wife," Isaac called out. "I know you can hear me. Please come in."

Rebecca gracefully entered the tent and knelt on one knee beside her sightless husband.

"Yes, my husband."

"Please sit, my dearest."

"Thank you, Isaac."

"Rebecca, I know you orchestrated this deception. Why did you not discuss this with me?" Isaac asked in a pained voice.

Rebecca was prepared for this moment. *I must break the news to him gently. Isaac loves Esau so. He is blind to Esau's evil, to his anger and fury. I myself do not know where it comes from.*

"Would you have listened to my words?"

"You are wise and kind-hearted. Your words are always of great value."

That is his polite way of saying no. I was right to deceive him. I must tread carefully. I must protect Jacob so he will fulfill the birthright. "The Elder shall serve the Younger."

"Esau is not the innocent that you imagine. He is not worthy of continuing your traditions."

"He is the eldest. He is a man of the world. Fulfilling the birthright requires a certain roughness; a capacity for leadership. Esau possesses these attributes - even more than I do, and more than Jacob."

He does not see. He does not understand. He is justifying his blind love for Esau. He should understand by now.

"Nonetheless, my darling, he can be cruel, even wicked." Rebecca retorted. "This is not our way. It is not your way. It is not what your father Abraham would have wanted."

"So now, my love, you are the interpreter of my father's traditions?" Isaac asked with some incredulity.

I must try a different angle. I must bring some proof and move him to action. He will not be persuaded with unverified accusations.

"Look at Esau's wives - they are idol worshipers! I am disgusted with my life on account of these daughters of Heth." Rebecca stated vehemently. "If Jacob takes a wife of the daughters of Heth like these, of the daughters of the land, why should I live?"

Isaac was taken aback by Rebecca's ferocity. For the third time in one day, he found himself confused and disoriented, surprised by each encounter, yet feeling greater revelation at each. He did not respond, but leaned forward, pensively looking at nothing.

Isaac could perceive that God's hand had been heavily involved in the day's events. Isaac had always presumed that Esau was the correct choice, yet God had clearly intervened. Jacob had shown great courage and skill in impersonating Esau.

And the blessing held. Isaac had felt the Divine Presence endorse the blessing. Jacob is truly blessed now. There must be some validity to the claimed sale of Esau's birthright to Jacob. The more Isaac thought about it, the more he realized that Rebecca was right. As much as it pained him, he realized Esau was not the one – it would be Jacob. The Elder shall serve the Younger.

Rebecca looked at Isaac's flowing features. His face seemed to contort with the emotions of his thoughts. *Have I pushed him too hard? How do we get past this?*

Esau was too rough, Isaac thought. However, he showed such tremendous respect to Isaac that it was a pleasure to have him around. The strong, confident, fearless son had been Isaac's hope for the future. But it was not to be. God had indicated as much.

Isaac held out his right hand to Rebecca. Instinctively Rebecca placed her hand in his. Isaac covered her hand with his left hand and gently caressed it.

"Love of my life," Isaac said softly, "why has it come to this? Why must you manipulate and scheme behind my back? Is there no trust between us? Is there no trust left in this family - in the descendants of Abraham?"

Small tears started to roll down Rebecca's face.

Oh Isaac. I love you so much! How do I explain my deception? How do I tell you about the secret prophecy I have carried for so long? How do I show you what you refuse to see?

"Despite our instructions and efforts, Esau has taken an evil path," Rebecca said softly. "It breaks my heart to see it. But we must remember our mission. We cannot forsake the God of your father and the kindness and goodness that he directs. Jacob is the one that will follow your path. The blessings you have now bestowed confirm that. Now we need to ensure he marries properly for the sake of the next generation."

"You have not answered my question," Isaac said as he tenderly wiped the tears he could not see from Rebecca's cheek. "Do you think I am so blind that I do not know my own children?"

Stubborn. Stubborn. He is focusing on the charade and not on what we need to do next. He has been deeply offended by the deception.

"I am sorry," Rebecca answered. "I did not see another way. Esau has always been your favorite. I did not believe you would change your mind just by my suggesting so. I could not take a chance that the wrong child would receive your blessing."

"What about trust? How can there be love, how can there be marriage or a relationship, without trust?" And now it was Isaac who shed tears.

He is in so much pain. Please God, help me! I do not know what to say anymore.

Isaac and Rebecca sat quietly, holding each other's hands.

"It is God's will," Isaac announced. "Perhaps my blindness is not only physical. This issue of the children has divided us for some time. We should never have chosen favorites."

Yes. Now you begin to understand.

"I showed too much affection and understanding towards Esau," Isaac continued. "The acts of the fathers are a sign for the sons. It seems I have repeated the mistake of another."

Just as Abraham accepted and justified Yishmael's behavior, you have turned a blind eye to Esau's.

"Isaac, we have both made mistakes," Rebecca explained, her hand still in his, "let us learn from them but not harp on them. Please do not doubt my commitment, dedication and love for you. I will do whatever is necessary to fulfill your life's work - even if it means deceiving you or hiding things from you."

Isaac faced her with his sightless eyes. "It must have been very difficult for you. You were very strong and brave to engineer and accomplish the ruse."

Thank You, God. He understands!

Isaac and Rebecca embraced and held on to each other silently. A chasm of many years had finally been bridged.

"Let us call for Jacob," Isaac stated. "I will re-confirm my blessings to him, this time aware of his true identity. I will direct him to find wives from your family and not from the daughters of the land."

Thank You, God! Thank You, thank You. Thank You. My mission is set and my love has returned to me.

Biblical Sources:

Genesis 27:28-29

28. So God give thee of the dew of heaven, and of the fat places of the earth, and plenty of corn and wine. 29. Let peoples serve thee, and nations bow down to thee. Be lord over thy brethren, and let thy mother's son's bow down to thee. Cursed be every one that curses thee, and blessed be every one that blesses thee.

Genesis 27:33-35, 41

33. And Isaac trembled very exceedingly, and said: 'Who then is he that hath taken venison, and brought it me, and I have eaten of all before thou came, and have blessed him? yea, and he shall be blessed.' 34. When Esau heard the words of his father, he cried with an exceeding great and bitter cry, and said unto his father: 'Bless me, even me also, O my father.' 35. And he said: 'Thy brother came with guile, and hath taken away thy blessing.

41. And Esau hated Jacob because of the blessing wherewith his father blessed him. And Esau said in his heart: 'Let the days of mourning for my father be at hand; then will I slay my brother Jacob.

Genesis 28:1-4

1. And Isaac called Jacob, and blessed him, and charged him, and said unto him: 'Thou shalt not take a wife of the daughters of Canaan. 2. Arise, go to Paddan-aram, to the house of Bethuel thy mother's father; and take thee a wife from thence of the daughters of Laban thy mother's brother. 3. And God Almighty bless thee, and make thee fruitful, and multiply thee, that thou may be a congregation of peoples; 4. and give thee the blessing of Abraham, to thee, and to thy seed with thee; that thou may inherit the land of thy sojournings, which God gave unto Abraham.

Secondary Sources:

Bereshit Rabbah 65:5

"*His eyes were dim*" (Genesis 27:1). By legitimizing the conduct of the evil Esau, he diminished his eyesight, for '*a gift blindeth them that have sight*' (Exodus 23:8) (and Isaac is viewed as having taken a bribe from Esau).

Bereshit Rabbah 65:17

Rebecca accompanied Jacob until Isaac's door and said, "I have done as much as I could for you. From this time forth, your Lord will suphold you."

"I am weary of my life because of the daughters of Heth" (Genesis 27:46). She conveyed fierce expressions of disgust.

Bereshit Rabbah 65:14; Eitz Yosef

Rebecca says to Jacob: "It will be binding upon me to intrude and say to your father, 'Jacob is honorable and Esau is evil.'"

Bereshit Rabbah 66:5

"Jacob was yet scarce gone" (Genesis 27:30). The gates flapped back. Jacob was poised behind the gate until Esau came in; then he exited.

Pesikta d'Rav Kahana 32:68

When Isaac wanted to bless Esau, he was not aware that Esau had set about on a path of evil. When Esau's actions were divulged to him, Isaac shook in apprehension of the Day of Judgment.

Bereshit Rabbah 67:2

"Isaac trembled very exceedingly" (Genesis 27:33) This exceeded his fear on the altar. He said, "Who is the person that became the intermediary

between the Holy One, Blessed be He, and me, to ensure that Jacob would acquire the blessings?" He said this of Rebecca.

Afterwards, God disclosed to Isaac that the blessing was indeed intended for Jacob.

Shocher Tov 105:4

"And the words of Esau her elder son were told to Rebekah." (Genesis 27:42) Who disclosed this to her? Prophetic Inspiration.

Rashbam Genesis 27:46:

Rebecca did not want to inform Isaac that Jacob's life was being threatened, so she exploited the inappropriateness of the Hittite women as an alleged reason for hurrying him away.

* * * * * *

Notes:

Though the text has Rebecca warning Jacob of Esau's murderous intent before she speaks with Isaac, I've excluded it from the story. She just as easily could have warned Jacob between the summons and his second blessing by Isaac. There's a principle that there isn't necessarily order in the narrative, especially when we are dealing with multiple and compressed scenes, characters and points-of-view.

[Vayetze]

(Genesis Chapters XXVIII-XXXII)

Jacob and Rachel
Julius Schnorr von Karolsfeld (1913)

The Shepherd's Kiss

"Be wary of Nerun," Laban called after Rachel. "He may try to use his larger flock to crowd you away from the well."

Rachel duly noted the warning as she herded her father's small flock of sheep towards the local well.

Rachel hummed a merry tune to herself as she slowly led the sheep along.

"Shaggy!" Rachel commanded with an authoritative voice while waving her staff, "Stay in line!"

A particularly hairy sheep immediately turned back into the formation of the flock.

From the distance Rachel could already spot three different flocks of sheep congregating around the stone-capped well.

That larger flock is obviously Nerun's. Rachel thought to herself. *I will be on guard. That speckled flock must be Shanar's; and those beautifully combed animals can only be those of kindly Zoab.*

Rachel was then surprised to see not three, but four men by the side of the well. Even from a distance Rachel recognized the outline and posture of Nerun and Zoab sitting and playing a game of backgammon. Shanar was sitting next to them whilst conversing with a stranger. Shanar gestured towards Rachel and the stranger looked at her from the distance.

Who is that stranger? I do not recognize him at all. And that red hair?! I thought only our family had red hair? He must be a descendent of Terach as well. Only Terach's descendents are noted for their red hair.

Shanar and the stranger then both started pointing at the massive stone covering the well.

Who can he be? Think girl, think! He must be of the descendents of either Lot or Abraham. The children of Lot are reputed as being fairly insular so I cannot imagine they would venture north of their territories. And it cannot be from the children of Ishmael. They all have much darker complexions. It must be one of Isaac and Rebecca's twins! It is clearly not the hairy brigand, Esau. It is Jacob!

Rachel started to flush with excitement. *Jacob, my cousin, had been mentioned as a potential match for me. But the distances had made the thought impractical. And now he is here!* Rachel looked herself over quickly, smoothed out her dress and combed back her hair with her hands. She knew that men were attracted to her, but she still wanted to look as best as she could. She continued towards the well, striding confidently with a bounce in her step, whistling a merry tune and radiating joy and beauty.

There was a small hill that obstructed her view of the well for a moment. And then she was there, facing him. Jacob looked into her eyes.

Their eyes connected like a shock of lightning that took Rachel's breath away. She could not believe that a mere look could have such an effect on her. She wanted to lose herself in those eyes. But then something in those deep eyes changed. And to Rachel's great surprise, instead of stepping closer, Jacob moved towards the well.

What is he doing?

Jacob quickly inspected the massive well-stone. He found sturdy handholds and planted his feet firmly in the ground.

He means to move the well-stone himself. He must be mad! It would take at least six grown men to move it. This is why the shepherds need to wait for everyone to come.

At first the stone did not move. By now Nerun, Shanar and Zoab were on their feet laughing at the foolish stranger. But then it moved. It moved ever so slowly. Jacob, with muscles bulging, gathered momentum and pushed the stone off the well.

Incredible!

Then as if Jacob had annulled the laws of nature, the well water rose towards Jacob.

He is truly a grandson of Abraham. He is mighty and God is with him.

Jacob took a nearby bucket, scooped water from the well and started to give water to Rachel's sheep.

Rachel had time to get over the initial excitement and look at Jacob more closely.

Why is he all alone? Why did he not come with gold laden camels as when his father sent for my aunt Rebecca? Look at his clothing! He is in rags. He is impoverished. Is that why he is acting so strangely? Is he trying to show his worth as a shepherd?

Jacob went back and forth wordlessly from the well to the sheep, making sure to give water to every last one of them.

I do not care if he is a pauper. If he will have me, I will be his. I will not leave him for as long as I live. I shall do whatever I can to marry this man!

As if in response to her thoughts, Jacob finished watering the sheep. He turned towards Rachel and without a single word gave Rachel a kiss. It was the kind of kiss on the cheek that cousins often give to each other. But this kiss was filled with such tenderness, such love and such longing that Rachel thought her heart would burst.

Oh my God. Jacob! What are you thinking? What will the other shepherds think? I know I love him, but he has not even introduced himself to me!

And then Jacob began to weep. It was as if he had read her mind or seen some tragic future. He was embarrassed. He was destitute. He was confused. He was lonely.

Do not worry, my love. Rachel thought to him looking back in his eyes. *You are safe now. We shall be together for as long as God allows.*

And then Jacob introduced himself to her.

Biblical Sources:

Genesis 29:1-12

1. Then Jacob went on his journey, and came to the land of the children of the east. 2. And he looked, and behold a well in the field, and, lo, three flocks of sheep lying there by it.--For out of that well they watered the flocks. And the stone upon the well's mouth was great. 3. And thither were all the flocks gathered; and they rolled the

stone from the well's mouth, and watered the sheep, and put the stone back upon the well's mouth in its place.—4. And Jacob said unto them: 'My brethren, whence are ye?' And they said: 'Of Haran are we.' 5. And he said unto them: 'Know ye Laban the son of Nahor?' And they said: 'We know him.' 6. And he said unto them: 'Is it well with him?' And they said: 'It is well; and, behold, Rachel his daughter cometh with the sheep.' 7. And he said: 'Lo, it is yet high day, neither is it time that the cattle should be gathered together; water ye the sheep, and go and feed them.' 8. And they said: 'We cannot, until all the flocks be gathered together, and they roll the stone from the well's mouth; then we water the sheep.' 9. While he was yet speaking with them, Rachel came with her father's sheep; for she tended them. 10. And it came to pass, when Jacob saw Rachel the daughter of Laban his mother's brother, and the sheep of Laban his mother's brother, that Jacob went near, and rolled the stone from the well's mouth, and watered the flock of Laban his mother's brother. 11. And Jacob kissed Rachel, and lifted up his voice, and wept. 12. And Jacob told Rachel that he was her father's brother, and that he was Rebecca's son; and she ran and told her father.

Secondary Sources:

Targum Yonatan, Bereshit Rabbah 29:9

An epidemic of the Lord afflicted Laban's sheep, hardly any remained alive. Laban dismissed his shepherd; the charge of the remainder of his flock was allocated to Rachel, his daughter.

Bereshit Rabbah 65:17

Both the arms of the Forefather Jacob were like two columns of marble.

Bereshit Rabbah 70:12

"He lifted up his voice, and wept." (Genesis 29:11). Why did he (Jacob) lament? He said, *"When Eliezer left to bring back Rebecca, it is written, The servant took ten camels* (ibid 24:10). *I, on the other hand, have not one ring or bracelet."* ... He lamented because he perceived that she would not be laid to rest next to him in the Cave of Machpelah... He lamented, since after he had kissed her, he noticed people gossiping to each other, for those in the east were austere [regardless of the fact that he had kissed her because she was part of his family (Hirsch)].

Bereshit Rabbah 70:16

Rachel was appreciated for her attractiveness.

Zohar 1:152a

When he (Jacob) watched the water swell up in front him, he realized that his companion would appear to him there.

Rachel's Gambit

Rachel put her shearing knife in her belt. She ran her fingers through the thick wool of the sheep as she stood listening to Jacob, who was standing amid his flock. She loved the rich scent of the docile animals.

"It's agreed then," Jacob told Rachel and her sister Leah. Leah; co-wife, partner, ally and sister all rolled into one. Now that Rachel had given birth to Joseph, the old rivalries and jealousies ebbed.

"We're leaving in the morning," Jacob continued. "Please pack your belongings and prepare the children. I don't know if we shall ever return to your father's house again."

The three of them glanced across the Aramean plains and looked at Laban's compound in the distance. Rachel recalled that before Jacob's arrival, it had been a simple mud-brick house. Now, twenty years later, it had grown into a stone mansion, with a series of smaller mud-brick houses and large stables. *It's all Jacob's work,* Rachel thought. *And father would steal it all over again.*

Rachel and Leah walked back to the compound silently with the sun setting in the distance. Rachel knew that Leah's dislike for their father mirrored her own. They were little more than slaves to him. And so was Jacob. Strong, honest, hard-working Jacob had built their father's wealth, but was still treated little better than a beast of burden. It was within the rules of their people. As long as Laban was the master, he owned them. Running away would not make them free. She knew Laban would chase them. He would bring his Idols in hand and demand they all return to him as per the Law.

The Idols, those abhorred Idols. She wondered if Laban controlled the Idols or if perhaps it was the other way around. She needed to get her hands on those Idols. She needed to remove the Idols from Laban's control and thereby sever the eternal bondage. Joseph must grow up free.

The sun sank below the horizon, with a full moon taking its place in the sky. As Rachel and Leah reached the compound they nodded to each other and separated to their private quarters.

Rachel walked past her own door and continued to Laban's private Temple. Laban is several days away, she thought. He would not have taken his Idols to the shearing of his distant flock. They must be here in his Temple.

Rachel walked to the back of the compound where the Temple stood. She blessed the full moon for lighting her path in the dark night. A wild black cat screeched suddenly. Rachel jumped back in fright.

"Damned cat," she murmured, shaking. "You scared me to death."

Rachel approached the Temple. It was a circular earthen structure, capped with a simple dome. The Temple's diameter was the length of two men, as was its height. Rachel remembered Laban lovingly building the structure himself, casting spells and protections for his Idols. The Temple's door was on the eastern side, to face the rising sun, with open windows at the three other points of the compass.

Rachel walked gingerly to one of the windows and peered inside. One lone, long candle burned brightly in a brazier hanging from the ceiling. On a stone pedestal in the center of the Temple Rachel could see the Idols. Both of them were on the pedestal. They were less than an arm's length in height. There was a golden statuette of a man, carved in exquisite detail, next to a matching silver one. If one looked at them long enough, one might think they were alive. That is not what troubled Rachel. It was the mastery they represented.

The holder of the Idols was the holder of their fortunes. It gave the right to land, to slaves and to flocks. The Idols were passed down from father to son. A freed Aramean man needed to receive his own Idol from his master. Laban would never release Jacob, nor would her righteous Jacob agree to accept an Idol for his release. By Aramean law, Jacob and his descendants would forever be slaves. Jacob did not care and would simply leave. But Rachel would not accept this. She did not want this doom hanging over her Joseph.

At the floor of the Temple a black sinuous form slithered around the pedestal. It had the thickness of a tree truck, and at some points Rachel was able to see through its body to the dirt floor underneath. *A demon*, she thought in alarm. *That is how he is protecting it. How can I get through it?*

Rachel found the head of the slithering form. Two bright red eyes shone from its face. It had neither nose nor ears. Just deep set eyes and a wide mouth that took up half its head. It reminded her of a giant eel, except that she could see long arms and legs at rest on the side of its body. The form shifted in and out of solidity proving its demonic source.

How can I trick the demon? Rachel wondered. *Catch it? Distract it?* What did she know about demons? Her father had never taught her the divinations, but he often liked to brag about how he captured them or controlled them. *Blood. Yes. They liked blood.* They were addicted to blood. They would follow the scent of fresh blood and feast on it. In gratitude they would obey your wishes.

Rachel retreated quietly from the Temple and scanned the ground carefully. Then she spotted it. The cat sat against one of the buildings, licking its paws. With a speed born of desperation Rachel pounced on the cat, with both arms outstretched. The cat eluded her right hand, but she caught the cat by the neck with her left. The cat screeched and scratched at Rachel's arm. Rachel smashed the cat's head into the ground, drew out her shearing knife and sliced the cat's neck. The blood flowed rapidly on the ground.

Rachel ran back to the Temple and stood behind the structure. A moment later the door to the Temple opened and the black demon slithered out. Rachel ran into the Temple. She stopped at the entrance, looking for further traps or defenses. She noticed a heavy layer of dust around the central pedestal. She took one light step forward and felt a burning sensation through her leather sandals. She pulled her foot back and looked closely at the floor. She saw the outline of footprints in the dust. She placed her foot on the footprint and felt no pain. She stepped on successive footprints and made it to the pedestal unharmed.

The golden Idol stared at her. It was beautiful. She had rarely seen a man-made object of such fine workmanship. Rachel grabbed the idol, only to cry in pain as the Idol seared the fingers of her right hand. She ripped the fabric off the bottom of her skirt, wrapped the woolen fabric around both idols and removed them from the pedestal. She backed away from the pedestal, careful to tread on the footprints again. She reached the doorway and breathed a sigh of relief.

As she turned and walked away a dark hand clutched her ankle and pulled her back to the Temple doorway. Rachel held on to the frame of the door, the Idols still wrapped and clutched in her left hand.

"You have deceived me, daughter of Laban," the Demon hissed from the ground.

"I fed you blood, Demon. Release me. That is my request."

"You think we're dumb, human? We are merely constrained. The blood drew me, but it was not enough to subjugate me. My task was to protect the Idols and I have failed. Though a thief, you are now the master of the Idols. But you will not leave unscathed."

"Then obey me, Demon. I am the master now. Release me and return to your circular vigil."

"I shall release you, but you have shamed me. For that you shall pay. No human may shame a demon and live long to tell about it. I place a death curse upon you."

"I fed you blood, I am the master of the Idols now; I am the daughter of your former master. How dare you curse me? Cease this absurdity right now and let me go."

"I shall let you go young Rachel. I shall even grant you a dying wish. Name your wish and I shall make sure it is granted before you die."

"I do not accept your curse, demon. Though if I could make one last wish before I die, it would be for another son."

"So it shall be. Now stand as I sing your doom."

The demon, still holding Rachel's ankle, curled his long body into a ball and looked at Rachel with his bright red eyes. He sang in a deep rumble.

"O, deceiver of the deceiver,
You have bested the son of Betuel.

Beautiful, youngest, Rachel,
The queen of he who shall be Yisrael.
Mother of warriors and kings,
Name forever revered.
Wealth and honor for your progeny,
Strife and battle with your sister's kin.
One more shall you see, child of sorrow,
Son of your right hand, son of strength.
Joseph shall rule an empire,
And hasten the exile.
You shall stand guard over your sons
On their long return home.
Not to see them in this world,
A power amongst the righteous."
The demon released Rachel's ankle.

Rachel walked back to her quarters, trembling. *I did it*, she thought. *I have the Idols. Joseph shall be free. Jacob and even Leah's children will be free. We must leave at first light before Laban finds out.*

But what about the death curse, she wondered.

Rachel smiled. *If the dying wish comes true, I will be satisfied.*

Biblical Sources:

Genesis Chapter 31:4-7, 9, 11-19

4. And Jacob sent and called Rachel and Leah to the field unto his flock, 5. and said unto them: 'I see your father's countenance, that it is not toward me as beforetime; but the God of my father hath been with me. 6. And ye know that with all my power I have served your father. 7. And your father hath mocked me, and changed my wages ten times; but God suffered him not to hurt me.

9. Thus God hath taken away the cattle of your father, and given them to me.

11. And the angel of God said unto me in the dream: Jacob; and I said: Here am I. 12. And he said: Lift up now thine eyes, and see, all the he-goats which leap upon the flock are streaked, speckled, and grizzled; for I have seen all that Laban doeth unto thee. 13. I am the God of Beth-el, where thou didst anoint a pillar, where thou didst vow a vow unto Me. Now arise, get thee out from this land, and return unto the land of thy nativity.' 14. And Rachel and Leah answered and said unto him: 'Is there yet any portion or inheritance for us in our father's house? 15. Are we not accounted by him strangers? for he hath sold us, and hath also quite devoured our price. 16. For all the riches which God hath taken away from our father, that

is ours and our children's. Now then, whatsoever God hath said unto thee, do.' 17. Then Jacob rose up, and set his sons and his wives upon the camels; 18. and he carried away all his cattle, and all his substance which he had gathered, the cattle of his getting, which he had gathered in Paddan-aram, to go to Isaac his father unto the land of Canaan. 19. Now Laban was gone to shear his sheep. And Rachel stole the teraphim that were her father's.

Notes:

Role of idols based on lecture at Machon Herzog that explained importance and prominence of master idols in Aramean culture and law, and therefore motivation of Rachel to steal them and that of Laban to chase Jacob for them.

Demonology based on Sforno and various Talmudic accounts.

Laban's magical powers based on his being identified with Bilaam the sorcerer.

Stealing of idols inspired by Indiana Jones.

[Vayishlach]

(Genesis Chapters XXXII-XXXVI)

The Birth of Rachel
Furini Fransesco (c. 1600-1646)

Death Pangs

"Push!" Yimeh, the midwife urged, "You must remain focused."

"There is no more strength in me," Rachel breathed heavily, "this child has drained my life."

Rachel was in birthing position on the bed in her tent. Bilhah and Zilpah held Rachel's arms on either side, while Yimeh was squatting at the foot of the bed, ready to catch the newborn should it succeed in exiting Rachel's swollen womb. Leah was running back and forth, preparing hot water, getting fresh cloths and doing anything to keep busy. Leah could not bring herself to be in direct contact with her dying sister.

Yes. Rachel was undoubtedly dying. Leah had seen the signs at the birthing-deaths of other women. Rachel's loss of blood during labor was severe. It was a miracle she had not died already, and that the baby was not stillborn. There was only hope for the baby now, though that too was diminishing quickly.

"Save your breath," Yimeh said more urgently to Rachel, "the only thing you need do in this world now is push."

"Call Jacob," Rachel pleaded weakly, "I must see him one last time before I die."

"I said stop talking!" Yimeh clamped the palm of her hand over Rachel's mouth. "Push! Do not speak! Push! Push! Push!"

Rachel was shocked by Yimeh's vehemence and awoke from her stupor. With renewed energy and concentration she started to push.

"That is it," Yimeh encouraged, "push in time with the urge."

In the meantime, Leah exited the tent to look for Jacob and at least fulfill her sister's dying wish.

"You are doing it," Yimeh reported, "the head is starting to descend."

"Aaargh!" Rachel screamed. "It is killing me!"

"Do not talk!" Yimeh clamped Rachel's mouth again. "Do not even scream. Use the pain to push. It is all about pushing now. There is nothing else in the world. Not pain, not limbs, not a baby, not even you. You must become a pushing machine, a pushing entity, for the next few moments. Push!"

Yimeh kept her hand on Rachel's mouth, stifling the next scream.

"I can see the head!" Yimeh exclaimed. "That is very good. Now is the critical part. Listen, Rachel. With the next urge, you must push with all your might. As if the entire world depended on it. I am taking my hand off now. Do not speak. Take a deep breath. Do not do anything else but push at the next urge with your entire being."

Rachel affirmed that she understood with a nod. She took a deep breath. Her eyes focused on nothing. Gritting her teeth and clenching the arms of Bilhah on her right and Zilpah on her left, she pushed.

"Yes! Now! Push!!" Yimeh yelled.

"Nnnggh!" Rachel grunted through her shut mouth.

"The head is out!" Yimeh proclaimed, as she tried to ease the baby out. "The hardest part is over Rachel. Just a few more pushes and you will be done."

"More?" Rachel asked incredulously, dazed from her last effort.

"Yes," Yimeh answered, focused on the baby. "Just two or three more pushes to get the rest of the body through."

"Hah!" Rachel laughed weakly. "I am surprised the last push did not kill me. You will have to do the rest of the pushing, Yimeh."

"You are not done yet," Yimeh retorted.

"This body is –" but Rachel inexorably started to push.

"Very good, Rachel," Yimeh calmly said as she supported the baby's head. "Save your breath and keep pushing. The first shoulder is out."

Jacob suddenly entered the tent with Leah right behind him.

He was shocked by the large pools of blood on the bed and the floor.

He stood silently, looking at the pained and dying Rachel, whom he now understood he would lose momentarily. He then looked at the head of the baby struggling to escape the dying womb. If Rachel did not succeed, it might very well be its tomb.

"Jacob!" Rachel shouted out as soon as she noticed him.

"Quiet!" Yimeh commanded. "Do I need to clamp your mouth again? The very life of this child depends on you not speaking. You must focus on the last pushes. My lord," Yimeh addressed Jacob, "please do not distract her. The life of your child hangs in the balance."

Death Pangs

Jacob moved to the back of the tent behind Rachel's view and quietly said to Rachel:

"I am here, my love. Focus on the labor and what Yimeh instructs you. I shall not leave you. Have no fear."

Rachel's answer was only: "Nnngh!"

"The second shoulder is out!" Yimeh called out joyously as she delivered the baby.

"Whaaaah!" the baby wailed before Yimeh even had a chance to give it the customary slap.

Yimeh expertly wiped the baby down and clamped the umbilical cord. She then wrapped the baby in fresh cloth and gingerly handed it to the dying mother.

"Have no fear, for this one, too, is a son for you," Yimeh said, knowing these last words were the account Rachel wanted to hear.

Rachel clasped the boy to her and cried tears of joy and of sorrow. She turned her head to look at Jacob. She thought back to their first meeting by the well. She thought of their history. She thought of all that went unsaid and undone between them. To the life that might have been. To the children she might have raised.

Clutching the boy to her chest, with tears streaming down her face, she used her last breath to name him. "He shall be called 'Son of my Sorrow' – Ben-oni."

Rachel then closed her eyes for the last time, still holding the boy tightly.

The tent was as silent as a grave.

Yimeh extracted the boy from Rachel's dead embrace and handed him to Jacob.

Jacob cradled him tenderly in his right arm, as wordless tears rolled down his beard.

"This is a day of deep sorrow for me," Jacob finally exhaled, "and for you my son. For you shall not know your mother, the love of my life. But your existence should not be further colored by sorrow. You are the last gift of my Rachel. Oh! My beloved, Rachel!" Jacob wept.

"'Son of my Sorrow' is not fitting for you," Jacob continued through his tears, "rather, you shall remain constantly by my side. You whose countenance is so much like my Rachel. You shall be named 'Son of my Right Arm' – Benjamin."

"Whaah!" was Benjamin's only answer.

Biblical Sources:

Genesis 35:16-18

16. And they journeyed from Beth-el; and there was still some way to come to Ephrath; and Rachel travailed, and she had hard labor. 17. And it came to pass, when she was in hard labor, that the mid-wife said unto her: 'Fear not; for this also is a son for thee.' 18. And it came to pass, as her soul was in departing--for she died--that she called his name Ben-oni; but his father called him Benjamin.

[Vayeshev]

(Genesis XXXVII-XL)

JOSEPH INTERPRETING PHARAOH'S DREAM
And Joseph said unto Pharaoh, The dream of Pharaoh is one: God hath shewed
Pharaoh what he is about to do... (Genesis 41: 25) *(41 14)*

Gustave Doré (1832-1883)

Joseph's Egyptian Attorney

"Execute the slave," Pharaoh intoned, while sipping delicately from his wine, "why need we be troubled by such a common case?"

"It is Potiphar's slave," the High Priest responded, "Potiphar himself requested the audience."

"Curious," Pharaoh replied, raising his eyes from his silver goblet, "let him in then."

A royal guard solemnly announced:

"The Grand Chamberlain, Potiphar."

Two other guards opened the tall, gold-encrusted doors to Pharaoh's public audience room.

Potiphar, who had been waiting in the antechamber, walked in slower than usual. He was often summoned to the hall for business purposes.

This was the first time he approached Pharaoh with such a sensitive personal issue. Potiphar noticed the rows of attendant priests sitting on either side of the hall. He saw the eunuchs standing with large palm branches at either end of the long, marble-encased chamber. They fanned constantly, making the spacious room significantly cooler than the sun-baked outdoors. Potiphar walked past columns with statues of previous Pharaohs and other figures from Egyptian history.

Potiphar approached the throne. At three paces distance he lowered himself to his knees and performed the customary obeisance. "Hail, Pharaoh! King and Lord."

"Hail, Pharaoh!" the priests rejoined, "King and Lord."

"Potiphar," Pharaoh motioned for him to rise, "why do you bother us with such a petty crime? Kill the slave and be done with it."

"It is not so simple, O Pharaoh," Potiphar cleared his throat, "I am not sure that the slave is guilty."

"We do not understand the problem," Pharaoh said in a perturbed tone, "your wife, The Grand Chamberlain's wife, accuses a lowly slave of accosting her and we are sitting here debating his innocence? Have him killed and get yourself a new slave."

"Will the Master of Justice," interrupted a priest from the side, "not seek out justice?"

"Who is this insolent dog?" Pharaoh asked the High Priest. "Can you not rein in your own priests?"

"I am but a humble servant," the daring priest continued with a perfect bow, "ready to serve Pharaoh in this case, that he may arrive at a wise and true resolution. Thus, all the subjects of his Kingdom will know yet again the divinity of his wisdom and power."

"Continue, priest," Pharaoh sat back, somewhat appeased.

"Potiphar's wife, Zelichah, has accused their household slave of accosting her. Potiphar himself seems unsure. It may be worthwhile to examine the claims further in order to arrive at a deeper understanding of the truth."

"Potiphar," the priest asked, "were there any witnesses to this supposed attack?"

"No."

"So it is his wife's word against the slave's," Pharaoh interjected. "It is clear we listen to the wife."

"That is unless, O Pharaoh," the priest continued, "there is reason to believe Zelichah is not telling the truth."

"Why should she lie about such a matter?" Pharaoh asked.

"O Son of Heaven," the priest waved dramatically, "Pharaoh, of all people, knows that all is not as it seems. Pharaoh can already sense that there is a mystery in this case, that only the brilliant mind of Pharaoh can uncover."

"Yes," Pharaoh cheered up, "you speak the truth priest. We shall bring light to the mystery, where no mortal can. We must determine what truly happened. It may not be as she claims."

"By making the correct inquiries," the priest continued, "by thinking as no mere mortal can, Pharaoh will reveal the truth."

"When did this theoretical attack occur?" Pharaoh asked Potiphar.

"Yesterday."

"Yesterday was the Overflowing of the Nile," Pharaoh thought out loud. "The entire kingdom was at the celebration at the river banks. That would explain why there were no witnesses. A convenient day for mischief."

"Does your wife bring any evidence of this attack?" Pharaoh pushed further.

"Yes," Potiphar answered. "She has the slave's garment that she claims he took off before his attack."

"That is a poor omen for him," Pharaoh stated, looking at the priest for guidance. "Why would the slave disrobe in her presence unless it was for dishonorable intentions?"

"We should examine his garment," the priest suggested.

"Yes. Excellent idea," Pharaoh exclaimed, "fetch the slave's garment."

"And hers also," added the priest.

"Hers also?" Pharaoh was confused. "Why do we require her garment?"

"Much may be learned from the fabrics that witnessed the true events," the priest explained.

"Of course," Pharaoh agreed. "Bring the garment she wore at the time of the reported attack," Pharaoh commanded a nearby guard. "Make sure you receive verification from someone else of the household, that they are indeed the correct garments. And be quick about it," Pharaoh added excitedly, "we gods do not have forever."

The guard rushed out of the hall.

"In the meantime, what else can we discover about the case?" Pharaoh asked, eager to make progress. "Where are your wife and the slave now?"

"In the antechamber."

"Wonderful!" Pharaoh clapped his hands with glee. "Who should we start with?"

"The slave," volunteered the priest.

"Why the slave?" Pharaoh eyed the priest suspiciously.

"Pharaoh already knows what Zelichah claims, but he has yet to hear the slave," the priest calmly explained. "Perhaps the slave will admit his sin, which will bring the case to a quick solution."

Pharaoh seemed mildly dejected by the thought.

"Or perhaps he will reveal some new information that only the insightful mind of Pharaoh will perceive. Pharaoh will then have the opportunity to probe his suspicions and re-examine Zelichah's claims."

Pharaoh nodded in agreement. "Call in the slave," he commanded.

Joseph walked into the hall wearing a simple slave's tunic. He looked curiously at the statues, and paused briefly by one as if in recognition. He continued to make his way towards the throne. All eyes looked impassively at Joseph. Most of all Pharaoh's.

"We requested the slave," Pharaoh asked in confusion, "who is this handsome princeling?" For Joseph indeed seemed handsome to Pharaoh, perhaps the most beautiful man he had ever

encountered. And he seemed to Pharaoh haunt-
ingly familiar.

"I am Joseph. Slave to Potiphar. I am a Hebrew, unrightfully brought from Canaan."

A murmur of incredulity stirred from within
the attendant priests.

"A Hebrew!" Pharaoh asked with a combination of repulsion and curiosity. "But so handsome?
You look more like a man of royal descent than a
slave."

"I am the great-grandson of Abraham, whom
you may recall visited your ancestor more than a
century ago."

"Abraham! Can it be?"

To everyone's surprise Pharaoh jumped out
of his throne and ran to Joseph. He took Joseph by
the arm, and forcefully dragged him back down
the hall, towards the entrance.

The surrounding guards quickly followed
their liege. The priests got out of their chairs and
followed the strange procession. The High Priest
and Potiphar caught up and stayed close to Pharaoh. The eunuchs stayed in their places, mechanically fanning the room.

Pharaoh stopped next to one of the female
statues and placed Joseph next to it.

"It is true! He is the spitting image of her!"

"Who is she?" Potiphar asked.

"That is the statue of Sarah. The legend is told that she was the consort of our predecessor, for a short while. She was considered the most beautiful woman in the world. It was our great-great grandfather that commissioned this statue of her as a reminder of her extreme beauty."

The assembled crowd kept looking at Joseph and back at the statue of Sarah. They were clearly related; their likeness certainly couldn't be coincidental. The fine shape of the nose. The clear brow. The high cheekbones. The almond-shaped eyes. The firm lips. Even the curl of the hair was identical.

"What a mystery indeed," Pharaoh exclaimed, "your accused slave is none other than Sarah incarnate! Why is everyone standing around? Back to your posts!"

"What was your name again?" Pharaoh turned to Joseph as the priests and guards skittered back to their places.

"I am Joseph, O Pharaoh."

"Yes, yes. Joseph. Let us continue with this investigation." Pharaoh strode back to his throne with Joseph; Potiphar and the High Priest were close behind. Pharaoh sat again with a regal flourish.

"Slave," Pharaoh addressed Joseph, "did you or did you not accost Potiphar's wife?"

"I did not accost my master's wife, O Pharaoh."

"Why does she claim otherwise?"

"I cannot say, O Pharaoh," Joseph glanced meaningfully at Potiphar.

"You know that the penalty for a slave attacking a master is death," Pharaoh explained. "If you do not produce a viable explanation, we shall have no choice but to execute you, as pretty as you might be, or as illustrious an ancestry as you may have."

"I could only guess the motivations of my master's wife in accusing me when I am blameless. However, were I to in turn cast aspersions upon her, it may dishonor my master who has been so good and kindly to me."

"Handsome and honorable," piped in the daring priest, coming back from the sidelines.

"True," Pharaoh noted, "but it does not help his case or chances of survival. He may be dismissed. Bring in Potiphar's wife!"

Joseph was unceremoniously escorted out of the chamber. A few moments later Zelichah walked in.

The royal guard formally announced: "Zelichah, wife of the Grand Chamberlain."

Zelichah glided into the hall in an austere and demure ceremonial gown. She bowed down next to her husband.

"Zelichah," Pharaoh motioned for her to rise, "why do you claim that your slave accosted you?"

"Because he did, O Pharaoh," Zelichah responded with a mixture of pride and pain.

"We have reason to believe that he may be innocent."

"Innocent? I have stated otherwise, O Pharaoh. That slave has been eyeing me since the day he arrived. He waited patiently until the house was empty, lured me into my bedroom and then attacked me. I have the evidence of his garment which I understand Pharaoh has so wisely summoned. I was his prey."

"Perhaps the hunted was really the hunter," the priest whispered to Pharaoh.

Pharaoh looked bewilderedly at the priest as he tried to make sense of his words.

"What woman could resist the extreme beauty we just witnessed?" the priest continued in an undertone. "Perchance there was truly an encounter yesterday between Zelichah and Joseph, but the roles were reversed."

"Prove it!" Pharaoh banged on his throne. "It is well and good to play at finding this slave innocent, but to accuse an important noblewoman of adultery is a dangerous game."

At that moment the dispatched guard returned with two garments in his hand. He approached Pharaoh with them.

"Divine timing," the priest said to himself. "O Pharaoh, if we were to ask the lady and the slave to wear their garments of the period in question, we may gain greater insight into the events."

"Make it so!" Pharaoh thundered, losing his patience.

The guard handed the dress to Zelichah who exited after him.

A few minutes later both Zelichah and Joseph entered the hall and walked towards the throne.

"Zelichah, if I may," the priest inquired, "why did you not participate in the celebrations of the Overflowing of the Nile yesterday?"

"I was ill."

"And is this your customary attire when you are ill? Your dress reveals more than it conceals. I believe that except for the eunuchs, no man here can help but be drawn by your obvious and overflowing beauty. O Pharaoh, this dress has one purpose only: seduction."

"That is no proof."

"True. But it is an indication. Let us examine further. You will also note that Zelichah's garment is in excellent condition, one that does not even hint at any violence. The slave's garment, however, is torn. You might argue that in his fit of passion, the slave tore his garment, but let us examine the tear carefully. O Pharaoh, if Pharaoh will, please clasp the slave's garment right by the rip."

Bemused, Pharaoh got off the throne, walked to Joseph and grabbed the garment at the tear.

"In the divine opinion of Pharaoh, could this tear have been self-inflicted?"

"No. The tear is in the back. He could not have reached it himself."

"That eliminates the possibility that the slave ripped his garment out of passion," the priest deduced. "Perhaps it caught on something, he tripped and then it ripped."

"That is not possible either," Pharaoh noted. "This garment was ripped by a human hand."

"Heavenly deduction, my dear Pharaoh! Then if he did not do it himself, and it was not an accident, and there was no one else in the house at the time, there is only one person that could have ripped that garment. Zelichah! The question now, however, is why? Was she ripping the garment in an effort at self-defense?"

"No!" Pharaoh exclaimed excitedly. "The tear was made by pulling away from the garment. That means the slave was moving *away* from the woman when she tore it. The slave is clearly innocent!"

"And the woman therefore is an ad–"

"Enough!" Pharaoh stopped the priest. "It is enough that the slave is innocent. We do not need to besmirch her name, nor that of her husband. Furthermore, this matter cannot be revealed, and the slave cannot go unpunished, lest others then discover the truth. What shall we do with him?"

"Let him sit in jail," the High Priest offered.

"Yes," agreed Pharaoh, "jail is certainly better than execution."

"Perhaps the royal jail," whispered the daring priest to Pharaoh, "this one requires close watch, someplace nearby."

Pharaoh nodded and signaled his secretary.

"We have decided that the slave known as Joseph shall be placed in our royal prison," announced Pharaoh with some pomp. "Word of this case, as gratifying as it was for us to solve, shall not leave this hall, on pain of death. Thus, truth is revealed, justice is served and the kingdom flourishes."

Pharaoh turned towards the priest, but he was no longer there.

"Where is that priest?" Pharaoh asked, not seeing him anywhere in the hall. All heads in the room turned to look for him, but the daring priest was nowhere in sight.

"Who was he?" Pharaoh then asked the High Priest.

"I do not know, your Majesty," replied the High Priest nervously, "we have never seen him before."

"That is a shame," Pharaoh answered nonchalantly, sipping from his wine again, "he would have made a good advisor."

Biblical Sources:

Genesis Chapter 3:6-15
6. And he left all that he had in Joseph's hand; and, having him, he knew not aught save the bread which he did eat. And Joseph was of beautiful form, and fair to look upon. 7. And it came to pass after these things, that his master's wife cast her eyes upon Joseph; and she said: 'Lie with me.' 8. But he refused, and said unto his master's wife: 'Behold, my master, having me, knows not what is in the house, and he hath put all that he

hath into my hand; 9. he is not greater in this house than I; neither hath he kept back any thing from me but thee, because thou art his wife. How then can I do this great wickedness, and sin against God?' 10. And it came to pass, as she spoke to Joseph day by day, that he hearkened not unto her, to lie by her, or to be with her. 11. And it came to pass on a certain day, when he went into the house to do his work, and there was none of the men of the house there within, 12. that she caught him by his garment, saying: 'Lie with me.' And he left his garment in her hand, and fled, and got him out. 13. And it came to pass, when she saw that he had left his garment in her hand, and was fled forth, 14. that she called unto the men of her house, and spoke unto them, saying: 'See, he hath brought in a Hebrew unto us to mock us; he came in unto me to lie with me, and I cried with a loud voice. 15. And it came to pass, when he heard that I lifted up my voice and cried, that he left his garment by me, and fled, and got him out.

Secondary Sources:

Tanchuma Vayeshev 5
The women of Egypt once congregated to gaze at Joseph's beauty. What was Potiphar's wife's reaction? She handed an etrog, and a knife

for peeling it, to each of them. She then called upon Joseph. As the women stared at Joseph's handsomeness, they dropped the knives and severed their hands. She said to the women, "If this is the way you are overcome when you look at him for only a moment, all the more so I, for I see him constantly!

Hizkuni

"There was none of the men of the house there within" (Genesis 39:11). Rabbi Yishmael commented: This was due to the Overflowing of the Nile, the ceremony of which everybody would partake, including the King and the officials; they would travel to behold and jubilate at the river.

Hizkuni

When Joseph was escorted to the king, the divine messenger Gabriel came disguised as a man, and requested the king to get the robes checked. If the woman's robe was torn, then it would be apparent that Joseph had advanced upon her, but if Joseph's robe was torn, then it would be clear that it was the woman who had assaulted him. The robe was checked; since Joseph's robe was torn, he was not condemned to die. Nevertheless, Joseph was not immediately released so that Potiphar's wife would not be publicly shamed that she assaulted Joseph. The advisors of Egypt authorized this judgment, and as a result, Joseph did not seize their territories during the period of famine.

Sefer HaYashar, Vayeshev
Potiphar's wife's name was Zelichah.

Midrash Agaddah, Bereshit
Joseph said, "You should be punished with death for buying me, for bondservants are from the Canaanite nations, when in fact I am the offspring of Shem and a scion of kings. King Pharaoh created a replica of Sarah. If this image does not bear resemblance me, then you are correct." They compared them, and Joseph's face matched the appearance of Sarah's image.

Bereshit Rabbah 87:9
Joseph's overseer said, "I acknowledge that you are innocent, but I am forced to imprison you in order to avoid causing a bad reputation for my children, for the folk will allege that she behaved in the same manner with others, and they will say that our offspring are not my own.

Destiny's Call: Book One - Genesis

[Miketz]

(Genesis Chapters XLI-XLIV)

The Cup is found in Benjamin's Sack
Henry Davenport Northrop (1894)

Benjamin's Fear

"That was not as terrible as I feared," Benjamin exhaled. "In fact, it was truly pleasant. The Viceroy was a gracious and generous host."

"Yes," Simeon added. "Even after he imprisoned me, I was treated as a royal guest."

Benjamin and his ten half-brothers were riding their grain-laden donkeys out of the Egyptian capital.

"The entire encounter was bizarre," Judah warned pensively. "The Viceroy's behavior was unusual. First he accused us of being spies, and when we brought Benjamin he treated us as long lost brothers. His line of questioning was also strange. Very personal. I think he was not convinced Benjamin is our brother. It was as if he was trying to ascertain our feelings towards Benjamin – why would he care?"

"Let us be thankful that we retrieved Simeon," Reuben counseled. "There is no need to seek further worries. Let us make haste back home to Canaan and put this episode behind us."

Agreeing with Reuben, Benjamin looked behind as if to say a final farewell to the capital. "What is that cloud?" he asked, perplexed.

It is moving towards us quickly, Benjamin thought.

All the brothers turned around.

"It is not good," Judah stated.

"It is an army," Simeon noted.

Yes. The rising dust of a quickly moving platoon. Benjamin's heart beat faster.

"Perhaps it is a troop redeployment?" Reuben said hopefully.

"No. It is an army in pursuit," Judah declared.

"Who are they after?" Benjamin asked nervously.

"Seeing as there are no other groups on this road that have entangled with the rulers, I suspect it may be us," Judah concluded.

"Let us run," Simeon urged.

"Our donkeys will never outrun their horses," Judah replied, "and we have done nothing wrong, though I am apprehensive. Form a perimeter around Benjamin, and let us continue casually."

"I do not need special protection," Benjamin protested weakly. *Will they sell me out at the first sign of trouble? My half-brothers have a history of treachery to the sons of Rachel.*

"I promised Father your safety," Judah answered. "If something were to happen to you, son of his favorite Rachel, Father would probably die from the grief. He would not take such news of the rest of us as badly."

Benjamin nodded his understanding as his brothers surrounded him on their mounts. *Judah is a man of his word; the rest might follow his lead.*

Moments later a cavalry one hundred men strong encircled them. They were led by the Viceroy's Captain, the young but authoritative Menasheh.

"Halt brigands!" Menasheh called as one hundred spears enclosed them.

"Why do you address us so, my Lord?" Reuben enquired.

"Why have you repaid evil to my master's generosity?" Menasheh retorted angrily. "You have stolen his precious drinking vessel. Did you not expect him to discover its absence? You have done wrong by him."

"Heaven forbid that your humble servants should do such a thing," Reuben replied. "We have already returned the money that was mistakenly placed in our bags. How could we take anything from your master's house, whether silver or gold? Search us! By whomever you shall find a stolen object we shall put to death, and the rest of us shall become your slaves."

"It shall be as you speak," Menasheh grinned, "though we shall not be as harsh as you suggest. Simple Egyptian justice shall suffice. The thief shall become my slave and the rest of you shall be free to go."

Reuben unloaded his heavy burlap bag from his donkey, placed it on the floor and opened it for Menasheh's inspection. Each of the brothers in turn repeated the gesture.

Menasheh dismounted from his proud Egyptian steed and, under cover of his cavalry's spears, approached the bags. He retrieved a short sword from his right side and thrust it into Reuben's open bag. Menasheh then swirled the sword in the bag, only to hear the swish of grain on steel.

Menasheh repeated the motions with each of the subsequent brothers: Simeon, Levi, Judah, Gad, Asher, Yissachar, Zevulun, Dan and Naftali. The brothers had relaxed, feeling that they were being proven innocent of this wrongful accusation. Judah was wary, sensing trouble.

Menasheh thrust his sword into Benjamin's bag. A "clink!" was clearly heard as metal hit metal. Menasheh plunged his hand into the bag of grain and triumphantly revealed the Viceroy's silver goblet.

The brothers gasped in shock. They tore their garments as a portrayal of grief. Benjamin was incredulous. Simeon whispered angrily, "thief, son of a thief! Just as your mother was a petty bandit, so have you turned out!"

Simeon has always been the roughest, Benjamin fought back his despair. *I cannot let him turn my other brothers against me.*

"Do not speak to me of chicanery," Benjamin hissed back. "Was I the one who sold Joseph into slavery? Who deceived our Father? Do not presume to show righteousness with me, Simeon. I am as blameless of this theft as I am of Joseph's sale. This is not my doing."

"I do not care to endure a family squabble," Menasheh interrupted. "You, Benjamin! Come with me. I shall be a firm master, my new slave. The rest of you are dismissed."

This is it. This is the moment of truth. Shall my brothers again betray a child of Rachel – shall they prove themselves to still be jealous half-brothers?

No one moved. The brothers looked at Menasheh blankly and then again at Benjamin. They did not react to the new situation.

"Are your brains addled, Hebrews?" Menasheh grunted. "Did you not hear me? Move away from the slave, so that I my take my lawful property. The rest of you are free to go."

Do not forsake me! Benjamin thought to his brothers. *If you leave me, we shall all perish! I will be enslaved, Father will die from heartbreak and the family will fall apart. Do not let the family of Israel end before it has begun.*

Menasheh motioned to his troops and the ring of spears became tighter around the brothers. Instinctively, the brothers encircled Benjamin in a closer formation, each with their back to Benjamin, facing the soldiers.

My brothers are with me. Benjamin felt hopeful.

Then an opening of spears was formed towards the north.

"Sons of Jacob!" Menasheh commanded. "You are now interfering in my business. Please leave my new slave. I assume you do not want to engage with my troops. Furthermore, if you ever want to purchase more grain from Egypt, I strongly suggest that you leave forthwith, with no further delay or resistance."

Do not leave me. Benjamin prayed. *Judah, please say something!*

"We shall all return with Benjamin," Judah stated, standing taller.

"That is not required or preferred," Menasheh replied, trying to hide a smile.

"Nonetheless, we insist," Judah reaffirmed. "We shall go together, or you will have a nice little brawl on your hands." At that all the sons of Jacob took a step forward, sword in hand. The spears moved back apprehensively.

"I will not risk harm to my new acquisition," Menasheh was taken aback by the Hebrew determination. "We shall escort all of you back to the Viceroy, where he shall lay his judgment."

With another motion of Menashe's hand, the spears parted way southward and closed in on the north side, pushing the brothers back to the city.

"We shall not abandon you," Judah whispered to Benjamin. "We shall never abandon you. We shall never again betray a brother." And then, in an undertone to himself, Judah continued, "I have made that mistake once already."

Biblical Sources:

Genesis 44:2-13

2. And put my goblet, the silver goblet, in the sack's mouth of the youngest, and his corn money.' And he did according to the word that Joseph had spoken. 3. As soon as the morning was light, the men were sent away, they and their asses. 4. And when they were gone out of the city, and were not yet far off, Joseph said unto his steward: 'Up, follow after the men; and when thou dost overtake them, say unto them: Wherefore have ye rewarded evil for good? 5. Is not this it in which my lord drinks, and whereby he indeed divined? You have done evil in so doing.' 6. And he overtook them, and he spoke unto them these words. 7. And they said unto him: 'Wherefore speaks my lord such words as these? Far be it from thy servants that they should do such a thing. 8. Behold, the money, which we found in our sacks' mouths, we brought back unto thee out of the land of Canaan; how then should we steal out of thy lord's house silver or gold? 9. With whomsoever of thy servants it be found, let him die, and we also will be my lord's bondmen.' 10. And he said: 'Now also let it be according unto your words: he with whom it is found shall be my bondman; and ye shall be blameless.' 11. Then they hastened, and took down

every man his sack to the ground, and opened every man his sack. 12. And he searched, beginning at the eldest, and leaving off at the youngest; and the goblet was found in Benjamin's sack. 13. And they rent their clothes, and laded every man his ass, and returned to the city.

Secondary Sources:

Bereshit Rabbah 84:20
Since Menasheh evoked the Tribes to rend their robes in despair over the matter of the 'stolen' chalice (when he pursued them and charged them of stealing it), his property was divided: half of his land was in Jordan and half was in Canaan.

Bereshit Rabbah 92:8
When the chalice of Egypt's governor was discovered in Benjamin's attaché, his brothers exclaimed, "Thief, son of a thief (in reference to Rachel, who stole Laban's idols)!" He retorted, "Is my lord Joseph here? Is the kid (that you butchered so that you could dip Joseph's cloak in the animal's blood) here? Brothers who bartered their brother!"

Bereshit Rabbah 95:1

When it came time for Benjamin to journey with his brothers to Egypt, they surrounded him and escorted him.

Tanchuma, Vayigash

When the chalice was discovered in Benjamin's attaché, each one of the brothers looked away. Who supported him? The brother that became an assurance for Benjamin: Judah.

[Vayigash]

(Genesis Chapters XLIV-XLVII)

JOSEPH MAKES HIMSELF KNOWN TO HIS BRETHREN

Then Joseph could not refrain himself before all them that stood by him . . .
And he wept aloud . . . And he said, I am Joseph your brother, whom ye sold into
Egypt . . . (Genesis 45: 1, 2, 4)   (45:1)

Gustave Doré (1832-1883)

Joseph Revealed

"We are all ready to be slaves to my lord," Judah stated, prostrating on the ground with his brothers.

"Nonsense," the Viceroy stated in a strange voice. "The man in whose possession the goblet was found," he pointed at Benjamin, "he shall be my slave, and as for you," he motioned to the rest of the brothers, "go up in peace to your father."

Why is he fixated on Benjamin? Judah wondered. *We just offered him eleven strong and valuable slaves, but he is only interested in Benjamin. There must be more to this than what we can see.*

"Please my lord," Judah raised his head from his kneeling position, "may your servant speak a word in my lord's ear – and let not your anger flare up at your servant – for you are like Pharaoh."

The Viceroy motioned for Judah to approach his chair.

I must make him understand the family dynamics, Judah thought. *If he keeps Benjamin, the remaining son of Rachel, Father will die! I cannot be the agent for yet another brother being enslaved. That would be too cruel a destiny.*

Judah quietly repeated to the Viceroy the recent family history and occurrences, adding how dear Benjamin is to their father, especially since the disappearance of Joseph, the first son of his beloved Rachel.

This Viceroy is powerful and smart, Judah noted to himself, *though he acts peculiarly. If he is intent on acquiring a slave from this mishap, I will offer myself.*

"If I return to my father," Judah pleaded, "and the youth is not with us – since his soul is so bound up with the youth's soul – when he sees the youth is missing he will die, and I will have brought down the spirit of our father in sorrow to the grave."

Judah paused a moment to catch his breath and see the impact of his words on the Viceroy. *I can sense his inner turmoil,* Judah thought hopefully, *and his eyes are becoming moist. I must press on.*

"For I took responsibility for the youth from my father saying, 'If I do not bring him back to you then I will be sinning to my father for all time.' Now, therefore, please let me remain instead of the youth as a servant to you my lord," Judah noted the Viceroy's gasp, "and let the youth go up with his brothers. For how can I go up to my father if the youth is not with me, lest I see the evil that will befall my father?!"

The Viceroy's eyes widened in surprise. *He is shocked by my willingness to trade places with Benjamin,* Judah concluded. *His face is bubbling and contorting...*

"Enough!" the Viceroy shouted, ripping his head ornament off.

"Servants! Leave the room!" the Viceroy continued shouting, his eyes wild.

Judah and his brothers were confused, not knowing what to do.

"You. Stay." The Viceroy pointed at the brothers, barely containing himself.

All of the guards and household staff scurried quickly out of the hall, perplexed by their master's uncharacteristic outburst.

As soon as the last servant closed the door to the hall, the Viceroy wailed: "Aaaaaah!"

The cry was loud, powerful and echoed the turmoil of a tortured soul. It reverberated throughout the Viceroy's mansion and beyond; it pierced the heart of whoever heard it. The brothers were stunned and confounded.

Who is this man? Judah wondered. *What have we unleashed?*

"I am Joseph," the Viceroy proclaimed through his sobs. "Is my father still alive?"

This is not possible! Judah thought in astonishment, *Joseph?! How can this be? After all these years?*

The brothers looked at each other with a mixture of fear and disbelief.

Can it be? Judah thought to the others, *Joseph? The one we betrayed? Now all-powerful in mighty Egypt? What does he want? Does he seek revenge? Is all this some ruse to punish us?*

Judah and his brothers took a step back in apprehension.

"Please come to me," Joseph called to them more softly, seeing their distrust.

"I am Joseph your brother," he said, controlling his tears, "it is me, whom you sold into Egypt. And now, be not distressed, nor reproach yourselves for having sold me here, for it was to be a provider that God sent me ahead of you. For these have been two of the famine years in the midst of the land, and there are yet five years in which there shall be neither plowing nor harvest."

Is this possible? Judah started to recover from his shock and examined Joseph more closely. *I now perceive some of his old mannerisms. But see how he has grown and matured. He is not the spoiled and vain*

*teen we cast off. He is still grandiose, but in a strong
and powerful way. God is with him!*

Joseph told the brothers about how his being
sold into slavery was part of a divine plan to save
the family from paucity. The brothers were apprehensive and unsure of Joseph's intentions.

"Hurry – go up to my father and say to him:
so said your son Joseph: God has made me master
of all Egypt. Come down to me; do not delay. You
will reside in the land of Goshen and you will be
near to me – you, your sons, your grandchildren,
your flock and your cattle, and all that is yours.
And I will provide for you there – for there will be
five more years of famine – so you shall not become destitute, you, your household, and all that
is yours."

He means to support us! Judah was surprised.
*He does not bear a grudge and he means to provide for
the entire family! This is incredible! Our distress has
been changed into salvation and joy; though some of my
brothers seem unconvinced. Joseph perceives this as
well.*

"Behold!" Joseph gestured towards Benjamin.
"Your own eyes see, as do the eyes of my brother
Benjamin, that it is I, your brother that is speaking
to you."

Joseph then approached Benjamin and embraced him tightly. Tears now streamed profusely down the cheeks of the reunited sons of Rachel.

He is Joseph! Judah affirmed to himself. *Joseph is back! God's hand is heavily at work here – how wondrous!*

Reuben was the next to hug Joseph, the elder who had tried to save Joseph all those years ago.

And then Joseph approached Judah. *It was my initiative to sell you,* Judah thought guiltily. *I am the one who created all this anguish.*

But Joseph's eyes were only filled with tears and love and forgiveness. He radiated to Judah: *You are forgiven my brother. All is forgiven.* And then they hugged.

Brother, they each thought as they warmly embraced.

Biblical Sources:

Genesis 44:14 – 45:15
14. And Judah and his brethren came to Joseph's house, and he was yet there; and they fell before him on the ground. 15. And Joseph said unto them: 'What deed is this that ye have done?

know you not that such a man as I will indeed divine?' 16. And Judah said: 'What shall we say unto my lord? What shall we speak? Or how shall we clear ourselves? God hath found out the iniquity of thy servants; behold, we are my lord's bondmen, both we, and he also in whose hand the cup is found.' 17. And he said: 'Far be it from me that I should do so; the man in whose hand the goblet is found, he shall be my bondman; but as for you, get you up in peace unto your father.' 18. Then Judah came near unto him, and said: 'Oh my lord, let thy servant, I pray thee, speak a word in my lord's ears, and let not thy anger burn against thy servant; for thou art even as Pharaoh. 19. My lord asked his servants, saying: Have ye a father, or a brother? 20. And we said unto my lord: We have a father, an old man, and a child of his old age, a little one; and his brother is dead, and he alone is left of his mother, and his father loves him. 21. And thou said unto thy servants: Bring him down unto me, that I may set mine eyes upon him. 22. And we said unto my lord: The lad cannot leave his father; for if he should leave his father, his father would die. 23. And thou said unto thy servants: Except your youngest brother come down with you, ye shall see my face no more. 24. And it came to pass when we came up unto thy servant my father, we told him the words of my lord. 25. And our father said: Go again, buy us a little food. 26. And we said: We cannot go down; if our youngest brother be with us, then will we go down; for we may not see the man's face, except our youngest brother be with us. 27. And thy servant my father said unto us: Ye know that my wife bore me two sons; 28. and the one went out from me, and I said: Surely he is torn in pieces; and I have not seen him since; 29. and if ye take this one also from me, and harm befall him, ye will bring down my gray hairs with sorrow to the grave. 30. Now therefore when I come to thy servant my father, and the lad is not with us; seeing that his soul is bound up with the lad's soul; 31. it will come to pass, when he seeth that the lad is not with us, that he will die; and thy servants will bring down the gray hairs of thy servant our father with sorrow to the grave. 32. For thy servant became surety for the lad unto my father, saying: If I bring him not unto thee, then shall I bear the blame to my father for ever. 33. Now therefore, let thy servant, I pray thee, abide instead of the lad a bondman to my lord; and let the lad go up with his brethren. 34. For how shall I go up to my father, if the lad be not with me? Lest I look upon the evil that shall come on my father.'

1. Then Joseph could not refrain himself before all them that stood by him; and he cried: 'Cause every man to go out from me.' And there stood no man with him, while Joseph made himself known unto his brethren. 2. And he wept aloud; and the Egyptians heard, and the house of Pharaoh heard. 3. And Joseph said unto his brethren: 'I am Joseph; doth my father yet live?' And his brethren could not answer him; for they were affrighted at his presence. 4. And Joseph said unto his brethren: 'Come near to me, I pray you.' And they came near. And he said: 'I am Joseph your brother, whom ye sold into Egypt. 5. And now be not grieved, nor angry with yourselves, that ye sold me hither; for God did send me before you to preserve life. 6. For these two years hath the famine been in the land; and there are yet five years, in which there shall be neither plowing nor harvest. 7. And God sent me before you to give you a remnant on the earth, and to save you alive for a great deliverance. 8. So now it was not you that sent me hither, but God; and He hath made me a father to Pharaoh, and lord of all his house, and ruler over all the land of Egypt. 9. Hasten ye, and go up to my father, and say unto him: Thus said thy son Joseph: God hath made me lord of all Egypt; come down unto me, tarry not. 10. And thou shall dwell in the land of Goshen, and thou

shall be near unto me, thou, and thy children, and thy children's children, and thy flocks, and thy herds, and all that thou hast; 11. and there will I sustain thee; for there are yet five years of famine; lest thou come to poverty, thou, and thy house-hold, and all that thou hast. 12. And, behold, your eyes see, and the eyes of my brother Benjamin, that it is my mouth that speaks unto you. 13. And ye shall tell my father of all my glory in Egypt, and of all that ye have seen; and ye shall hasten and bring down my father hither.' 14. And he fell upon his brother Benjamin's neck, and wept; and Ben-jamin wept upon his neck. 15. And he kissed all his brethren, and wept upon them; and after that his brethren talked with him. 16. And the report thereof was heard in Pharaoh's house, saying: 'Joseph's brethren are come'; and it pleased Phar-aoh well, and his servants.

[Vayechi]

(Genesis Chapters XLVII-L)

Joseph Embalmed
Henry Davenport Northrop (1894)

The First Anti-Semite

"Father," the boy asked, "why is that coffin made out of metal? I thought they are usually from ceramic or wood?"

"That is discerning of you my son," the father answered, as they followed the funeral procession. "This is a special coffin for Joseph, the old Viceroy."

"Why is his so different then?"

"You shall see soon enough. His burial will be different."

"And there are so many people here. I have never seen such a large crowd for a funeral before."

"Yes, it is large indeed. I think Jacob's funeral, the Viceroy's father, might have been this big, though his family has grown significantly since then."

"What family, Father?"

"Why, the Children of Israel. They have multiplied at an astonishing rate."

"You say it like it is a bad thing."

"I do not think it is good that strangers should become so powerful. It was worrisome enough when the Viceroy had such strong control of Egypt."

The procession continued towards the Royal burial grounds.

"And who are those old men carrying the coffin?"

"Those are the Viceroy's brothers and his two sons."

"The Royal honor guard seems more armed than usual, and there are many soldiers."

"That is very perceptive of you, my son. That is very good. It is always important to take note of all the details. I suspect those guards may be called upon shortly."

The brothers wished to enter at the gateway to the Royal burial grounds, but the honor guard directed them towards the river instead.

The procession stopped for a moment. When the brothers realized the guards had the advantage, they continued towards the river.

"You see, my son. Sometimes just a show of force is sufficient to prevent the use of force, and can spare wasteful violence."

"Yes, Father. For a moment though, I thought there would be a fight."

"That was a risk. But the Hebrews are smart. They would not fight over this matter."

The procession approached the banks of the Nile, with the honor guard closely directing the brothers with the coffin to the shore.

"Where are they going to bury him, Father?"

"In the Nile."

"In the Nile? That is so strange. I have never heard of such a thing. Why in the river?"

"To make his body less accessible."

"Less accessible? Less accessible to who? For what?"

"Let us say that it would be less than convenient if his family were to have easy access to his remains."

"But why? I thought the old Viceroy did great things for Egypt. I learned that he had single-handedly saved the empire from starvation. This does not seem like an honorable burial."

"Hmmm. They should stop teaching fabricated history. Joseph may have done good things for Egypt in the past, but he was still a Hebrew. Besides, he did those things in his own self-interest as well. He had been a lowly imprisoned slave before the previous Pharaoh elevated him, and invited his entire family to move to Egypt – and to the best land."

The procession reached the water and the brothers, under the watchful eyes and spears of the honor guard, solemnly lowered the coffin into the river.

Hoards of Hebrews rushed to the shore, to look at the rapidly sinking coffin. They all pointed and looked at each other. They looked at the surrounding trees and road and at the landscape on the other side of the Nile, as if they were trying to memorize the exact location.

"I do not understand, Father," the boy continued, "the Hebrews have always been loyal, if not outstanding Egyptian citizens. I know that many of the grandchildren of Joseph remain in royal service and they are usually the best administrators and most fearsome soldiers."

"Nonetheless, my son," the father explained as he surveyed all the Hebrews at the shore, "they are foreigners. They are not our friends and you would do well to remember that. They have always remained aloof from us Egyptians and our culture. They look down upon our gods, our worship and practices. And those Hebrews that do embrace our ways – they are the worst! They try so hard to ingratiate themselves into our circles, but they are nothing but two-faced traitors. I fear them the most!"

"Yes, Father. I understand and hear what you say. Then we must find a way to protect ourselves from these Hebrews. They are so numerous!"

"We shall have to devise a way. Now, with the Viceroy gone, it will be easier. But it will take time and patience. The other brothers are no less intelligent than old Joseph was, though perhaps not as sophisticated in the ways of government."

"As you say, Father."

"Son, you are old enough to call me by my formal name. You must become accustomed to this."

"Yes, Pharaoh."

"Do not forget that these Hebrews are a threat. Perhaps the greatest threat the empire will face. I will set the wheels in motion, but it may very well be you who will have to face them head on."

"Yes, Pharaoh. I shall not disappoint you."

Biblical Sources:

Genesis 50:26

26. So Joseph died, being a hundred and ten years old. And they embalmed him, and he was put in a coffin in Egypt.

Secondary Sources:

Tractate Sotah 13a

The Egyptians built a metal casket; they submerged it into the Nile River in order to sanctify the waters. Moses approached and positioned himself on the edge of the Nile. He called, "Joseph, Joseph, the time has come for the pledge of the Holy One, Blessed be He, that He would deliver you; the time has come for fulfilling the promise that you made to the nation of Israel. If you appear, good; if you don't, then we are absolved from our pledge." At that moment Joseph's casket rose to the surface.

How did Moses apprehend Joseph's location? Serah, the daughter of Asher, divulged it to him.

Devarim Rabbah 11:7

They made a casket that weighed 500 talents; the sorcerers cast it into the river. They said to Pharaoh, "Do you wish for this nation to never leave? If they cannot find the bone's of Joseph, they will nevermore be capable of leaving."

Zohar 1:222b

His casket was lowered into a river; there it would not turn out impure.

Midrash Hagadol, end of Bereshit

Moses held Joseph's chalice and sculptured four parts out of it. On one piece he carved a lion, on the second an ox, on the third an eagle, and on the fourth a man. Then he approached the Nile, cast in the carving of the lion, and said, "Joseph, it is now time for the nation of Israel to be delivered," but the casket did not surface. He cast in the carving of the ox and then that of the eagle, but the casket did not surface. Lastly, he cast in the carving of the man and stated, "Joseph, the time has now come." Joseph's casket immediately rose to the surface, and Moses carried it off.

Shocher Tov 81:7

The sons of Joseph were not subjugated in Egypt, they also did not "rest on a cauldron of meat." Instead, they were armored guards and soldiers.

Shemot Rabbah 1:4

When Joseph was still alive, the nation of Israel did not experience the affliction of Egypt (i.e., subjugation). But once Joseph passed away, the hardship was put upon them.

Tractate Eiruvin 53a

"Now there arose a new king over Egypt, who knew not Joseph." (Exodus 1:8). He feigned that he did not know.

Questions for Discussion

The Forge of Music

1. What are the parameters of forgiveness in this story? Comment on the idea that both Lemech and Yuval must seek forgiveness.

2. Music can be a powerful tool. What is your relationship with music?

3. The theme of sight runs through the story. Who is to blame for Lemech's blindness?

4. Is creativity always met with suspicion? Why is Lemech so opposed to Yuval's music at the beginning of the story?

5. Is the end of the story realistic? Does Lemech seem to be the type of father that can tolerate change and development?

Tower of Egotism

1. What role does fanaticism play in this story?

2. Why do you think Nimrod wanted Mebtah's two bricks? What do they represent?

3. Is the Tower ultimately finished? Will Nimrod regret his decision?

4. The title of the story, Tower of Egotism, reflects Nimrod's approach to leadership. Rename this story to represent a better leader with a better outcome.

5. Nimrod's other lieutenants are only too happy to take Mebtah's place. Why?

Oath-Brothers

1. Do you believe Eshkol is motivated by faith or by greed?

2. Can you think of examples of modern-day oath-brothers?

3. Do Eshkol, Mamre and Aner consider the God of Abraham to be their God? Who do they place their faith in?

4. Do you, as an individual, feel responsible to the larger community?

5. Has fear ever stopped you from doing something? What?

Escape from Sodom

1. Who is the true tragic hero in this story – Lot, Edis, their daughters or the people of Sodom?

2. Where is God in this story?

3. Was Edis correct to criticize Lot as being a weak character? Do we ever see Lot as being a leader?

4. The angels seem to lack compassion or words of warmth for Lot and his family. Is this consistent with your view of angels?

5. Justify Edis' choice to turn around.

Reconciliation

1. Imagine the development of Isaac and Ishmael's relationship from this point on. Can you envision a time when they could be friends?

2. In childhood, Isaac and Ishmael were never encouraged to be friends. Would Abraham be pleased with his sons' reconciliation?

3. Imagine what Ishmael had been doing since his departure from Abraham and Isaac.

4. Isaac says to Ishamel: "I think that if it had been solely up to Father, he never would have banished you. God gave him a direct command." Is Isaac implying that Abraham disagreed with God's instruction?

5. Ishmael claims that he ceded his rights as Firstborn through his sinful past; even penitence wouldn't rectify this loss. If he repents, could he regain his former status?

Questions for Discussion

Rebecca's Crisis

1. Discuss which character deserves the most sympathy.

2. Describe a scenario where you have used duplicitous ways to get the correct outcome.

3. Do the ends ever justify the means?

4. Rebecca orchestrated Jacob taking his brother's blessing. How does she decide when to be proactive and when to sit back demurely? Do you agree with her strategies?

5. Why doesn't Rebecca just tell Isaac the prophecy she received? How does this story help define their relationship?

The Shepherd's Kiss

1. Jacob dazzles Rachel with his strength. Where does his strength come from?

2. In the span of a few short minutes, Rachel falls in love with Jacob. Is love ever that simple and pure?

3. It is clear what Rachel sees in Jacob. Describe the scene from Jacob's perspective.

4. Jacob is at one of his lowest points when he meets Rachel. Comment on his tears when meeting Rachel.

5. Jacob and Rachel were not the only two people in this story. What were the shepherd's thinking?

Rachel's Gambit

1. Rachel and Leah were married to the same man (Jacob). Discuss the pros and cons of polygamy.

2. Rachel and Leah essentially desert their father on the grounds that he mistreated them and their families. Did the level of his mistreatment warrant their leaving, or did they transgress the commandment to honor one's parents?

3. Laban worshiped idols – as was common practice in his time. Has idol worship been completely eradicated from our generation? Discuss.

4. Rachel confronts a demon, who curses her. Do demons, angels or other spirits have any influence in our lives?

5. Was Rachel justified in interfering with her father's idol-worship?

Death Pangs

1. Rachel's life certainly didn't turn out the way she had imagined when she first fell in love with Jacob at the well. Was her death a tragedy or a triumph?

2. Is Jacob dishonoring his wife by renaming their child?

3. How important is a name? What is the story behind your name?

4. Imagine the retelling of this story to Benjamin as he grows older. Describe his parent's relationship to him.

5. The midwife comes across as an unsympathetic character (she certainly knows that Rachel is about to die). Is her lack of compassion and pushiness just the opposite?

Joseph's Egyptian Attorney

1. Joseph's beauty is commented on numerous times throughout the story. How does beauty play a role in advancing Joseph's story?

2. Joseph sees his great great-grandmother's statue in Pharaoh's court. What must he feel like seeing Sarah's image in the court?

3. Joseph is silent throughout most of the story. Imagine what must be going on in his mind while he is standing before Pharaoh.

4. Comment on the unknown priest who speaks up in Pharaoh's court. What role does he serve for Pharaoh? Why is he important in telling this story?

5. Potiphar's wife often comes across as a woman scorned. Can you find more complexity in her personality?

Benjamin's Fear

1. One of the overriding themes of this story is trust. Where do you see trust between the brothers? Where is it missing?

2. Both Reuben and Judah serve as leaders of this small group. Who do you feel is the true leader?

3. Most of the brothers seemed to have learned their lesson after their betrayal of Joseph. Who has not? And is he justified in seeming so angry?

4. There have been many Biblical stories about the betrayal of brothers. There are far fewer stories about the protection of a brother. Discuss other brothers that have been betrayed in Genesis.

5. Would history have taken a different course if the brother's had indeed betrayed Benja-

min and allowed him to be taken back to Egypt?

Joseph Revealed

1. Simeon's reaction is left out of this narrative. Imagine Simeon's reaction to Joseph's revelation.

2. Why doesn't Joseph join them in bringing Jacob down to Egypt? He must want to see his father as soon as possible.

3. Joseph still seems to be a bit arrogant in his interaction with his brothers. Has he not learned his lesson? Is there an appropriate time for arrogance?

4. Discuss the role of forgiveness in relationships. Are there times in your lives when you have been called upon to forgive as generously as Joseph?

5. Imagine the relationship between Joseph and his brothers in 10 years time. What would that family dynamic look like?

Questions for Discussion

The First Anti-Semite

1. This story is based on a conversation between father and son. Is this how prejudices are passed down? Recall a conversation your parents had with you, either good or otherwise, that made an impression on you when you were young.

2. Why don't the Children of Israel insist on a proper burial for Joseph? Why do they accept the Egyptian's insistence that Joseph be buried in the water?

3. Imagine what Joseph's eulogy must have been. Try to recreate an Egyptian's eulogy for Joseph and a eulogy given by one of his sons.

4. Where else has water been significant in the story of the Jews in Egypt?

5. If this is the first instance of anti-Semitism, can there be lessons learned for the future?

Essay: Biblical Motivation

We're at war. It is an ancient war. It is a war of ideas and belief and culture. It goes as far back as the Hellenists foisting Greek culture upon the Hebrew nation. Many embraced the exciting, intoxicating wines that emanated from Athens. However, Jerusalem could not long absorb such foreign influences without ill effects. Those that embraced Hellenism wholeheartedly were quickly lost to their brethren. Those that fought it took up arms and joined the Maccabees in their famed rebellion. But what about those in the middle? What about those who enjoyed only certain aspects of Greek wisdom and culture? There were certainly some developments of the Greeks that were worthy of adoption, were there not? Maimonides himself freely borrowed from their famed Aristotle (though there were many in his own day that frowned upon him for that).

Today the war continues and the battle-lines are as muddled as ever. There is a global culture popularized by the studios of Hollywood. It is a culture that permeates almost every aspect of modern life. Commercialism, advertising, product design, technology and materialism are all touched by the values of the ancient Greek gods of beauty, eternal youth, wealth and power. Our brothers who revel or wallow in the wine of modern culture are as lost to us as the former Hellenists.

In contrast, as a rebellion against these influences, many communities have cut themselves off from modern life. Walls of fear and xenophobia surround their self-centered communities. However, their walls are cracked. Fear was never a protection against the Other. It merely leads to Hatred, Misunderstanding and eventually Dysfunction.

And what about those in the wide middle? Those dedicated to higher values, to the eternal truths of generosity, kindness, integrity, wisdom, honest work, reverence of elders, respect of others, charity, depth, tradition, service and community. Modern culture does pay lip service to such values. But it often seems merely window dressing to the driving values of the false gods we worship instead.

Essay: Biblical Motivation

Those of us in the middle are tossed about like lone sailboats on a tempestuous sea. We reach for beacons in the distance, but are ever confused as to which one leads to safe harbor. The glitzy glamorous visions attract us like moths to a flame. From what values can we receive warmth without getting burned?

The tools and technology of modern culture are clearly powerful and perhaps irresistible. For children who cannot otherwise sit still, to be mesmerized and transfixed by the latest electronic stimulation of mind-numbing nonsense is a victory of modern innovation. Even the beautifully written books of adventure, conflict and excitement that draw children and adults into their world, while valuable as a source of entertainment, do little in the educational realm.

That is where we enter the realm of Biblical Fiction and my motivation to jump into the fray. As a believer in the importance and even the primacy of the Bible, I cried at my children's ability to memorize fictional inanities in stark contrast to their disinterest in their very own rich Biblical tradition and culture. The attraction of modern entertainment was clear and obvious. The dusty Bible remained on the bookshelf, unopened and unused. It was boring. It was not interesting.

Even the most exciting stories were told in an archaic, ossified fashion.

One of the most successful storytellers of the last century was J.R.R. Tolkien. In "The Lord of the Rings" Tolkien created a world filled with a deep history, so rich, so detailed, so seductive, a realm real and exciting and ready for successive exploration by a worldwide audience.

We have such a history! And it is true! We have a document lovingly protected, painstakingly transmitted, and punctiliously maintained which is millennia old! And it is OURS! It is not of make-believe elves and orcs and dwarves and hobbits, no matter how cute or inviting they may be. We have a history, a tradition, a story of Man himself. From the very beginning of time. From the foundation of History. The story of Adam. The story of Noah and the Flood. The story of the Patriarchs: Abraham, Isaac and Jacob. Of the Twelve Tribes of Israel. Of the Exodus from Egypt. Of Moses and the Commandments. And much more.

Until somewhat over a century ago, the word of the Bible was considered sacrosanct. It was taken for granted that the stories and histories were real. Then something changed. Doubt. Doubt in our traditions. Doubt in the chain of teacher to student and father to son. Was it the disruption of modern life? Modern wars? Faith in God was replaced by Faith in Science, though that science was determined by High Priests in white cloaks that were just as fallible as their religious counterparts.

But how do we turn back the clock? How do we return this tradition to the center? One way is to fight fire with fire. To use the very tools, the very weapons, technology and media of our amorphous enemy. Many have paved the way. They have written Biblical Fiction. They have taken those biblical stories, the bones of the ancient texts and laid new muscles and sinews upon them. They have given them skin and clothing to make them palatable, understandable and accessible to a modern audience.

To aid the Biblical Fiction writer, besides the basic text itself, there is a strong written tradition of biblical commentary that has accompanied the biblical text for almost as long as the prime text itself. This commentary has been kept by the People of the Book, by the Jewish people, all along its long exile and to this very day. The commentary is often as exciting, as revealing, as controversial as the prime text itself, if not more so. It paints a clearer and often a more complex picture of different biblical personalities and stories. This commentary is part of the Jewish tradition.

Of course, these authors all come with their own voice and style, but I will split them into three broad categories for the purpose of this essay. There is a school of writers that use the biblical stories and personalities as a springboard for the telling of their story. They have taken the bare bones of the textual information and mangled their skeletal creations. They have developed crippled and misshapen beings with little semblance to either the texts or the traditions that accompany the biblical stories. They may be successful and entertaining, but I believe it is a disservice to students or potential students of the Bible.

The second school of writers is truer to the sources, but may use their storytelling to promote certain agendas. It may be a parochial religious ideology it is espousing. It may be supportive of biblical criticism that erodes belief in the divine inspiration of the Bible. While this school is not directly offensive it is perhaps the more dangerous and insidious of the two. It is easier to be defensive against a clearly incorrect depiction of tradition than against one that is only mildly so.

The third school of writers comprises those who are true to the sources and tradition. These are not surprisingly those most familiar and intimate with the extensive biblical commentary. I humbly place myself within this category. Throughout my writings, I have toiled to become familiar with as many of the relevant commentaries for each personality and story as possible. I have read both the basic text and the commentaries in their original Hebrew. I have visited the archeological sites of the setting for many of the stories and perused through the latest archeological studies and theories. I have become as intimate as possible with the biblical texts, geography, findings, and commentaries until the point where I can almost picture the scene in my mind's eye, as if Abraham were standing in front of me now. Over thirty years of loving study and research have led to my constructing a world that exists in my mind. A world based on the Bible and its commentaries.

It is still a fictional world though. It is made up. I have weaved the stories in such a way that it may be difficult for the casual reader to differentiate between biblical dialogue and my own, between biblical commentary and novel exegesis, between archeological evidence and fantasy.

At the end of the day, I also need to entertain, to tell a good story. I may also be guilty of the sins of the other two schools, of either mangling a character or promoting my own parochial agenda, but I suppose that is the protection we all share by the title 'fiction'. I have been aided and inspired in this effort by many great and authoritative people. Any and all errors are of course my own.

My hope, my fervent desire, is that these stories will just be the beginning of your journey. That your curiosity will be piqued. That you will wonder, what is based upon the text and what is fictional? That you will want to visit the primary sources and see for yourself what it says. Why do these personalities hold such an important place in our tradition? What else does the Bible say? What other mysteries, adventures and revelations are hidden within its pages? That you too may discover the beauty, the passion and the guidance that I have found in it.

Ben-Tzion Spitz
Alon Shvut, Israel

September 2011
Elul 5771
Around 3680 years since Abraham walked upon these hills.

Thank You!

No man is an island and there is no possible way I could have ever completed such a task or have even considered it without the encouragement and assistance of family, friends and a team of professionals. Here is where I attempt to thank as many of you as I can recall.

To God, who gave me the interest, abilities and wherewithal to even consider such a project.

To my wife, Tamara. She is the beginning and the end. She is my constant inspiration, helpmate, best friend, conscious, cheerleader, censor, better judgment and so much more.

To my eldest, Eitan. My biggest fan and prime audience. If he likes it, it makes the cut.

To my children, Akiva, Elchanan, Netanel, Yehoshua, Yehuda and Tiferet. A fantastic audience for my stories. For some reason they like the bloody ones best.

To my parents, Elliot and Nira Spitz, for the unflinching support of all my efforts, and to my mother who still checks my spelling and still finds mistakes.

To my in-laws, Josef and Gita Tocker, for there constant support and assistance, and my father-in-law for his unending graphical assistance including the breathtaking cover of this book, the really cool Valiant logo and the enhancement and layout of the maps, timeline and genealogies.

To my siblings, Boaz Spitz, Ilana & Daniel Epstein, Kalman Spitz and Jennifer Kahen, for their feedback and encouragement.

To my friend, partner and editor, Dr. Avi Shmidman of Bar-Ilan University. His consistent and wonderful editing and advice has raised the standard of my writing and the quality of what you hold.

To Rabbis Assaf Bednarsh, Yitzchak Blau and Gad Dishi. Each in their own way has given me fantastic encouragement, inspiration, assistance and has been a significant resource in finding or validating many rabbinic commentaries and sources.

To Devorah Katz for the Questions for Discussion section.

To Judy Labensohn for her writing coaching.

To Elana Greenfield for her writing workshop.

To Fern Reiss for instruction on the ins and outs of the publishing world.

Thank You!

To Rachelle Chazen for proofreading, assembling the index, glossary and all the publishing assistance.

To Rachel Nachmani for the beautifully drawn maps.

To the many Rabbis, teachers and friends at Yeshivat Har Etzion, Machon Herzog, the community of Alon Shvut, Yeshiva University, Yeshivat Kerem B'Yavneh and elsewhere. Over the years they have expanded my knowledge and familiarity with the texts and commentaries, have introduced me to the latest archeological digs and findings or most precious of all, have given me feedback that has encouraged me and that has improved my writing. These include, but are not limited to: R' Aharon Lichtenstein, R' Yehuda Amital z"l, R' Moshe Lichtenstein, R' Yaakov Medan, R' Baruch Gigi, R' Gideon Perl, R' Yosef Zvi Rimon, R' Mordechai Friedman, R' Moshe Taragin, R' Menachem Leibtag, R' Doniel Schreiber, R' Jonathan Mishkin, R' Yaakov Beasley, Dr. Yael Ziegler, Shani Taragin, Mali Brofsky, R' Alex Israel, R' Joshua Amaru, R' Yoni Grossman, R' Yossi Elitzur, David Nativ, R' Avi Wolfish, R' Yoel Bin-Nun, R' Chanan Porat, Jeremy Brody, Yonatan Shai Freedman, Egbert Pijfers, Peter Weiser, Elie Gertel, Dovid Schwartz, Dr. Shmuel Katz, Aryeh Lustig, R' Mitchell Orlian, R' Alan Schwartz, R'

Avraham Rivlin, Phil Chernofsky, R' Shalom & Rachel Berger, R' David Debow, my Biblical Fiction students from Midreshet Emuna Ve'Omanut, and many more.

There were many other teachers and people who influenced my Biblical education over all the years of my instruction. A couple that stand out include R' Yaakov Benzaquen of Caracas, Venezuela. I still recall how while teaching my 4th grade he straddled his desk and pretended he was riding a horse in simulation of Joshua's spies on their mission to Jericho. He brought the Bible to life. The second teacher is Prof. Chaim Sober of Yeshiva University. He taught a series of courses on the Ancient Near East that placed the Bible in a regional, political and cultural context of the times when it was written and took it out of the vacuum in which it was classically taught to us. He made it more real and tangible.

To all the subscribers to my email list. The weekly deadline forced me to write. I'm not sure it would have happened otherwise.

And finally, to you, the reader. Thank you for your time and attention. It is appreciated.

Index of Biblical Sources

All Biblical Sources are in the Book of Genesis

Escape from Sodom

Chapter 19: Lot escapes Sodom

Reconciliation

25:8-10: The burial of Abraham in the Cave of the Patriarchs

Rebecca's Crisis

25:21-26: The birth of Esau and Jacob
27:1: Isaac's blindness
27:28-30: Isaac blesses Jacob instead of Esau
27:33-35: Esau discovers that Jacob took his blessing
27:41: Esau plans to kill Jacob
27:46: Rebecca disapproves of Esau's wives
28:1-4: Isaac blesses Jacob again

The Shepherd's Kiss

29:1-12: Jacob meets Rachel

Rachel's Gambit

Death Pangs

Joseph's Egyptian Attorney

Benjamin's Fear

Joseph Revealed

44:14-45:15: Joseph reveals himself to his brothers

The First Anti-Semite

50:26: Joseph's burial

Glossary of Biblical References

A

- Abraham – Patriarch and Forefather of the Israelites.
- Aner – One of three Amorite confederates of Abram in the Hebron area, who joined his forces with those of Abraham in pursuit of Chedorlaomer, king of Elam.
- Amrafel – A king of Shinar (Babylonia, broadly speaking) who invaded the west along with Chedorlaomer, king of Elam, and others, and defeated Sodom and the other cities of the plain in the Battle of the Vale of Siddim.
- Aram - Region located in central Syria.
- Arameans - A Northwest Semitic semi-nomadic and pastoralist people who originated in what is now modern Syria.
- Asher – Jacob's eighth son, blessed with prosperity.

B

- Bilhah – Rachel's handmaid and wife of Jacob; mother of Dan and Naftali.
- Benjamin – Jacob's twelfth son. Most beloved of Jacob after disappearance of Joseph.

D

- Dan – Jacob's fifth son, described as a snake in the blessing of Jacob.

E

- Esau – Isaac's oldest son, Jacob's twin brother, progenitor of the Edomites.
- Eshkol – One of three Amorite confederates of Abram in the Hebron area, who joined his forces with those of Abraham in pursuit of Chedorlaomer, king of Elam.

G

- Gad – Jacob's seventh son, blessed to return to his territory safely after war in the blessing of Jacob.
- Gemorah – One of two cities, immersed in impenitent sin, that God destroyed.

- Goshen – A province of Egypt.

H

- Hebron – originally a Canaanite city before it became one of the principle centers of the Tribe of Judah.

I

- Isaac – Abraham's son; one of the three patriarchs of the Israelites.
- Ishmael – Abraham's firstborn son, born of Abraham's marriage to Sarah's handmaid Hagar.

J

- Jacob – Isaac's son, Esau's twin brother, one of the three patriarchs of the Israelites.
- Joseph – Jacob's eleventh son, sold into slavery by his brothers. Became the most powerful man in Egypt next to Pharaoh.
- Judah – Jacob's fourth son, known for his extraordinary physical strength.

L

- Laban - Son of Bethuel, brother of Rebecca and the father of Leah and Rachel.
- Leah – Matriarch. The first of Jacob's wives, Rachel's sister, and mother of Reuben, Simeon, Levi, Judah, Issachar and Zebulun.
- Lemech - Sixth generation descendant of Cain; his father was named Methusael.
- Levi – Jacob's third son. His descendants became the Priestly caste of Israel.
- Lot – Abraham's nephew; notable episodes in his life include his travels with his uncle Abraham and his flight from the Kingdom of Sodom.

M

- Mamre – One of three Amorite confederates of Abram in the Hebron area, who joined his forces with those of Abraham in pursuit of Chedorlaomer, king of Elam.
- Machpela Cave – the cave of the Patriarchs that Abraham originally purchased for the burial of his wife, Sarah.
- Menashe – Eldest son of Joseph. Became one of the 12 Tribes together with his brother Ephraim.

N

- Naftali – Jacob's sixth son, known for his speed, commended for giving goodly words in the blessing of Jacob.
- Nile River - A major north-flowing river in North Africa.
- Nimrod – Son of Cush, credited with building Tower of Babel, and was King of nations in the Fertile Crescent.

P

- Pharaoh – Title used for ancient Egyptian rulers of all periods.
- Potiphar – Captain of Pharaoh's palace guard.

R

- Rachel – Matriarch. The favorite wife of Jacob, and mother of Joseph and Benjamin.
- Rebecca – Matriarch. Wife of Isaac and the mother of Jacob and Esau.
- Reuben – Jacob's eldest son, known for his sense of responsibility, characterized as fickle and condemned to dwindle in power and size in the blessing of Jacob.

S

- Sarah – Matriarch. Wife of Abraham and the mother of Isaac.
- Sodom – One of two cities, immersed in impenitent sin, that God destroyed.
- Simeon – Jacob's second son, known for his wrath. His descendants were condemned to become divided and scattered in the blessing of Jacob.

T

- Terach - The father of the Patriarch Abraham.
- Tuval-Kayin – Son of Lemech, half brother of Yuval.

Y

- Yissachar - Jacob's ninth son, known for his religious scholarship.
- Yuval – Son of Lemech, half-brother of Tuval-Kayin.

Z

- Zevulun - Jacob's tenth son, known for his commercial activities and financial success.

- Zilpah - Leah's handmaid and wife of Jacob, mother of Gad and Asher.
- Zoar - One of the five cities of the plain of Jordan which escaped the "brimstone and fire" which destroyed Sodom and Gomorrah, for having sheltered Lot and his daughters.

About the Author

Ben-Tzion Spitz is the author of a blog, Torah Shorts (at ben-tzion.com), where he has published dozens of biblical fiction stories and biblical analysis based on ancient, medieval and contemporary sources. He has been exploring and researching biblical stories and archeological findings for over two decades. He is also the creator and lecturer of the Biblical Fiction series in Jerusalem, Israel.

He lives in Alon Shvut, Israel with his wife and their seven children.